INFLATA

Terry Ravenscroft

Copyright © Terry Ravenscroft, 2011

Cover by Tony Colligan

A RAZZAMATAZZ PUBLICATION

About the author

The day after Terry Ravenscroft threw in his mundane factory job to become a television comedy scriptwriter he was involved in a car accident which left him unable to turn his head. Since then he has never looked back.

Before they took him away he wrote scripts for Les Dawson, The Two Ronnies, Morecambe and Wise, Alas Smith and Jones, Not the Nine O'Clock News, Ken Dodd, Roy Hudd, and several others. He also wrote the award-winning BBC radio series Star Terk Two.

Born in New Mills, Derbyshire, in 1938, he still lives there with his wife Delma and his mistress Divine Bottom (in his dreams).

Also by Terry Ravenscroft

STAIRLIFT TO HEAVEN
STAIRLIFT TO HEAVEN 2 - FURTHER UP THE STAIRLIFT
STAIRLIFT TO HEAVEN 3 - ALMOST THERE
CAPTAIN'S DAY
FOOTBALL CRAZY
IT'S NOT CRICKET!
JAMES BLOND - STOCKPORT IS TOO MUCH
I'M IN HEAVEN
THE RING OF THE LORD
SERIAL KILLER
DEAR AIR 2000
DEAR COCA-COLA
DEAR PEPSI-COLA
SAWYER THE LAWYER
LES DAWSON'S CISSIE AND ADA
THE RAZZAMATAZZ FUN EBOOK
ZEPHYR ZODIAC
CALL ME A TAXI
GOOD OLD GEORGE
DEAD MEN DON'T WALK
THE RAZZAMATAZZ NOT ENTIRELY PC ENCYCLOPEDIA

CHAPTER ONE

For the first few years of his life Hugh Pugh, the Secretary of Trade for Transport, had been quite fond of his name. He liked the sound of it, the rhythm of it, Hugh Pugh, it was like a little rhyme all of his very own. It was not until he commenced school at the age of five that he began to dislike it. For his classmates didn't see his name in the same way Pugh did, as a little poem, but as an object of fun, their cruel young minds immediately homing in on its phonetic possibilities and coming up with hurtful nicknames like Hugh Poo and Hugh Phew.

By his ninth birthday he had begun to like it again. By then he had learned from his father, a dyed-in-the-wool member of the Labour Party, that he had been named after the great Labour leader Hugh Gaitskill. Already a Labour supporter even at that tender age, having been thoroughly schooled in the dogma of Socialism by his father, it had made him very proud.

Since that day in the long ago Pugh had experienced good days and bad days. Today was a bad day. And things would soon be getting worse. Much worse. The next general election, hanging over his head like a dark cloud, was only months away - probably May, but subject to the Prime Minister's whim – and following it he would be out on his ear along with about a hundred other Labour MPs, if the opinion polls were to be believed.

As things stood at the moment he was just about able to keep his head above water on his ministerial income, plus what he was able to fiddle on expenses, which wasn't half as much as it used to be thanks to the goose that laid the golden egg having been killed off in the 2010 crackdown. Over the past thirty odd years, during the process of going down the well-trodden path from bright-eyed idealistic young party worker to grasping Member of Parliament, he had also gone through three expensive divorces and now bore the ongoing maintenance costs this entailed. Three of his offspring were being educated at private schools, which didn't help matters. If that wasn't enough he had the latest in a string of high maintenance girlfriends to keep fed, clothed, shoed and watered.

Pugh's office, in the Marsham Street premises of the Department of Transport, was as devoid of taste as it was opulent. It was the room of someone who, with a very large amount of money to spend, had been intent on spending as much of it as he possibly could. Nothing stated this to more effect than the carpet.

Carpets had always signified class to Hugh Pugh. When he was a boy people who were better off than his parents had carpets. They were the first thing his young mind had recognised as a status symbol. One of his schoolmates had a carpet in the living room; his dad was a foreman at the bike factory. His Uncle Alf and Auntie Nellie had two carpets; Uncle Alf was a solicitor's clerk. The Pugh's home, a two up two down terraced house in the suburbs of Nottingham, didn't even have one carpet; the living room floor was covered by cheap linoleum and a peg rug. Pugh had vowed that when he grew up, got married and had a house of his own he would have a carpet as good as anyone.

He kept his promise, and on becoming a Member of Parliament had extended it to include the carpet of his office. With easy access to the means by which to fund the purchase of carpets his various offices had benefited from a fine carpet ever since. The higher the position in Government he had attained, the more sumptuous the carpet he had demanded. His present carpet, a specially commissioned Axminster in browns and greens, had a pile well over an inch thick.

The wallpaper, which Pugh didn't particularly like, and had only purchased because it was more expensive than Derry Irvine's, had a pattern similar to the brown aerial roots of the mangrove tree on a background of green foliage. Pugh's secretary Myra had once remarked that the journey from his office door to his desk was like going on safari.

In a corner of the office, adding to the jungle effect, stood a ceiling-high rubber plant. To demonstrate his wit to the many visitors to his office Pugh had hung several condoms from the plant's branches. Not a single visitor had laughed. The nearest thing to a laugh was a sort of curled-lip smirk from the Deputy Prime Minister, which could have been indigestion. The Minister for Children, who at the time had a larger than usual bee in her bonnet about under-age sex, had actually scowled at him when he had pointed out the rubber plant's rubber crop. Pugh had put it down to their lack of a sense of humour.

On the wall in front of him, at either side of the door, two blown-up framed photographs reminded Pugh of his past and his present, where he was and where he was now. His past was represented by a black and white snapshot of him as an eight-year-old, standing on the front doorstep of his home, wearing his first ever Labour Party rosette. Depicting his present was a photograph of him shaking hands with the Queen. Looking at them now Pugh reflected bitterly that if there had been a photo on the wall illustrating his future it would be perfectly blank, or at best a huge question mark.

Seated at his large desk, which along with his chair was fashioned from an oak tree purloined from Sherwood Forest, the first thing he had ordered on becoming a fully-fledged Minister five years previously, at Environment, Pugh now considered his position for the tenth time that morning.

There was no doubt he would be defeated at the next election; unlike his ample bottom he had only a marginal seat. His majority of under a thousand would not so much be eaten away, more hungrily gobbled up, if the eight per cent swing predicted by the opinion polls was only halfway accurate. Four per cent would be more than enough. How on earth was he supposed to manage, when his income had been snatched away from him, if he could barely manage now? It didn't bear thinking about it; the decline from plenty to poverty would be unbearable. There would be a generous ministerial pension of course, about half his current salary he reckoned, but munificent as this was it wouldn't amount to anything like the amount he was clawing in at the moment.

He might of course be able to work himself onto a Quango or two, which would bring in some extra money. The earnings wouldn't be peanuts, especially if he could manage to get himself appointed chairman and thus gain access to the loot. But it was a big might. Although there was a lot of 'you scratch my back and I'll scratch yours' between the main political parties, with the best will in the world Pugh couldn't see his own back being scratched very much as the Conservatives hated him to a man. Calling their leader 'The Oxford Abortion', in his occasional column in the *Guardian*, hadn't improved matters. Still he'd said it now, what's done was done, no use worrying about it, you can't put the shit back in the donkey.

A spell as an MEP would be the thing. You only had to

look at Neil Kinnock. The ex-Labour leader hadn't looked back since he'd managed to work himself onto the European gravy train. Top paid job after top paid job, Commissioner of This, That and the Other, he was better off than he'd ever been, certainly far better off than he'd ever been as Leader of the Opposition. The same for his Welsh bit of a wife.

But no one knew more than Pugh that a job in Europe was just pie in the sky, given his record over the last few years, for no one had spoken out against the European Union more vociferously than The Right Hon Hugh Pugh.

In reality he had no strong feelings about the EEC either one way or the other. However, an even greater and much more significant reality was that his constituency had over the last couple of years absorbed more than its fair share of emigrant Poles; Poles whom his constituents saw as a danger to their job prospects and consequentially to their living. With an eye on nothing more than the next general election, and the votes that these constituents had in their gift, no one had spoken out louder than Pugh about the influx of Europeans invading our shores, infesting our neighbourhoods and stealing our jobs (after first satisfying himself that there were still more of the indigenous population living in his constituency than there were of Poles).

Many ministers on retiring write their memoirs. But Pugh couldn't see the world of literature bolstering his pension pot. He had already approached four publishers and none of them had shown the slightest interest. He scowled as he recalled this. It would have been different if he'd have been Posh bloody Spice or some other so-called 'celebrity'. The bastards would have been queuing up with their million pound advances. *"A book of your favourite Australian outback roadkill recipes, Kylie? Get scribbling immediately!"*

The Lords was another source of potential income. But when he had hinted to Phil that he wouldn't be averse to accepting a peerage in the next honours list the Prime Minister had as usual skirted around the subject, hadn't given him a direct answer yea or nay. The second time Pugh had brought it up it was the same story. It was only at the third time of asking, when he had insisted on an answer, that Phil had informed him he didn't hold out much hope that a seat in the upper house would be anything more than an outside possibility; he would clearly do his best, but there were only so many peerages he could dole out without the media jumping on him and his next list was oversubscribed already.

Pugh scowled again on recalling the meeting. Well bollocks to Phil, and bollocks to a peerage too, the thought of having to turn up at the House of Lords every day in order to qualify for the lousy three hundred quid a day appearance money and sit with those old wankers who daily disgraced its chamber made him almost as depressed as the prospect of not having enough money to live on.

He sighed deeply and looked out of the window. The view from his top floor office was uninspiring. Not that he expected that looking out through the window would give him inspiration. Hugh Pugh was not the sort of man who could be inspired by views, unless they were views of the insides of restaurants and wineries. He would give you ten views of the Lake District's Derwent Valley seen from Latrigg for one of the kitchens at *The Fat Duck* or the cellars of Chateau Latour.

At least it was Friday. Tonight he would be able to get the hell out of London and hightail it up the motorway to spend the weekend in his Derbyshire constituency, exchange the noise and grime and sleaziness of the capital for the peace and tranquillity of the countryside. Which isn't to say that he ever spent much time in the actual countryside, the countryside of leafy trees and rambling streams, of verdant meadows and winding lanes. The many and varied walks in the hills and dales to be found on his doorstep held no attraction for him whatsoever. However within the many little villages to be found in those hills and dales were welcoming oak-beamed country pubs with even more welcoming bits of skirt who didn't mind dropping their knickers for a powerful, important politician.

The extent to which women were attracted to men who held power had never ceased to amaze Pugh. Henry Kissinger had been spot on when he said that power is the ultimate aphrodisiac. The opposite sex was certainly impressed more with power than they were with good looks, if Pugh knew anything about it. Indeed if it came to a straight contest between himself and a good-looking young man as to which of them would be the first to bed a beddable young woman he would lay odds on himself any day of the week.

Thinking about this he regarded the life-size bronze bust of himself on his desk. He had three more such busts, specially commissioned when he first rose to the heights of Cabinet Minister. One was in the windowsill of his study in his Derbyshire cottage. Another was on a pedestal in the entrance hall of his London town house, looking down imperiously on all who entered. The third had been intended to grace a retreat in the south of France. However the planned retreat had never materialised, through lack of funds, and the way things were looking at the moment it wouldn't be all that long before it retreated altogether.

The face of the bust bore what Pugh liked to think of as an expression of guarded benevolence, but had more accurately been described by more critical observers as 'like a bulldog chewing a wasp'. As he looked at it now it confirmed to him that it couldn't be his good looks that supplied him with a steady string of bed partners, for he was indeed no oil painting. From a certain angle and in uncertain light he bore a striking resemblance to Andrew Lloyd Webber. He certainly had Lloyd Webber's heavy jowls - a feature which he could happily have done without, but not at the expense of reigning in an appetite for the type and quantity of food that could only encourage heavy jowls. Along with Lloyd Webber's bushy eyebrows he shared the peer's indeterminate hair style, although not its colouring; Pugh, rather than resort to the dye bottle, preferred to leave it in its natural grey state, fondly imagining that it made him look distinguished. And of course the famous composer lacked the distinctive scar that Pugh had on his top lip, a campaign wound in more sense than one, which he had received when he had been unfortunate enough to kiss the only six months old baby in his constituency who possessed a full set of teeth, and with which, showing admirable judgement, it had bit him.

In many respects Pugh was similar to John Prescott; unfaithful, uncouth, occasionally obnoxious, and, like the former Deputy Prime Minister, a man who had been promoted far beyond his abilities as a sop to the trades unions and the far left. People who go line dancing would be more suitable for office.

A difference between Prescott and Pugh was that the latter could put together a sentence in which the words were more or less in the right order. A further dissimilarity between the two heavyweight politicians was that Pugh didn't have two Jaguar cars at his disposal, and had therefore not been christened 'Two Jags' by the press. He did however have two cars, and was well aware that the only reason he hadn't been named 'One Merc One Beamer' by Fleet Street was because the expression sounded a bit awkward, even by the standards of the British press.

The most notable similarity Hugh Pugh had to John Prescott was that he was a self-made man. Like Prescott he had not made a very good job of it. Good enough to drag himself off the shop floor of the Nottingham bike factory in which he had toiled since leaving school at fifteen to become the union's youngest ever shop steward at the age of twenty; good enough to be voted onto the city council four years later; good enough to become a county councillor in another four years; good enough to stand for and win a seat in Parliament at the second attempt at the age of just thirty three; and good enough now, at the age of fifty five, to be a Minister in Her Majesty's Government.

But not good enough, whilst in the process of doing all this, to have insulated himself against future bad times, to have feathered his nest, or at least feathered it enough to withstand the loss of his parliamentary salary when the country next gave its verdict at the ballot box. For in tandem with his rise through the ranks from shop steward to Cabinet Minister had come an appetite for good living; the forsaking of the pints of beer of his early days as an MP in favour of the expensive bottles of wines of the Cote d'Or and Bordeaux; the switch from fish and chip suppers or Chinese and Indian takeaways to dinner several times a week at *The Ivy* and *Le Gavroche*; the casting off of ready-to-wear suits from Montague Burton in favour of bespoke suits from the tailors of Savile Row; the exchange of Saturday afternoon at the football match for Saturday night at a West End theatre or a top London nightspot; and although he had yet to replace cricket with croquet it was felt by many observers that it was only a matter of time.

Reflecting on his problems he sighed again. It was all right for the other lot, the hairy-arsed, the Conservatives, and the Liberal Democrats to a certain extent; when they got booted out of Parliament they just walked into a job, some cushy number or other, pausing only to add another couple of directorships to the half-dozen or so they already held down courtesy of being a Member of Parliament. It was different for Labour MPs. Especially ones like himself, who didn't have any cronies in industry who could offer him one of the sinecures they distributed to their own with no less abandon than if they were throwing confetti at a wedding.

Things might have been different, maybe the future would have held out a little more hope for Hugh Pugh, had he possessed any particular skills that could be offered to the world of commerce in exchange for filthy lucre; it is by no means unknown or even uncommon for Labour Members of Parliament to hold directorships in industry. However the only skill Pugh had acquired during his years as an MP was the art of keeping his head just enough above water to keep on being an MP, which is of course the prime consideration of all MPs.

On his way up to Cabinet Minister level Pugh had also held the position of Junior Minister at Health, at Education and at Culture. In common with the vast majority of politicians he had known nothing about the job he had been put in charge of before being put in charge of it, and even less about it when he had left it in order to jump back on the merry-go-round that would drop him off at the next job he knew nothing about. On the re-opening of Parliament following the general election of 2010 a BBC television reporter had commented that whilst awaiting the start of the swearing-in of new Members of Parliament Ceremony all the new MPs were simply milling around without knowing quite what was going on, without knowing quite what they were doing. Nothing that has happened before or since would lead anyone to believe the situation will ever be otherwise.

It was this total lack of expertise in anything other than being a politician that was Pugh's problem. The only job he had ever held down was as a machinist at the local bike factory, a place of employment where he had in fact machined the same bicycle part as the actor Albert Finney when he starred in the role of Arthur Seaton in the groundbreaking kitchen sink film *Saturday Night and Sunday Morning*. However Pugh was aware that the ability to machine a bike part was unlikely to impress the board of a bicycle manufacturing company enough for them to offer him a directorship, even if they still made bicycles in Britain.

He knew this to be true because years ago, on first becoming an MP, he had let it be known to one such manufacturer that he had very close connections with the industry; in fact he had once been employed in the very same job as that performed by Albert Finney in *Saturday Night and Sunday Morning*. Much to his delight the imparting of this information had struck pay dirt immediately.

"You don't say?" the cycle manufacturer had said, obviously impressed. "I may have just the job for you, Mr Pugh."

Could it be that easy? "Really?" he said, scarcely able to credit his good fortune.

"If you'd be interested of course?"

"Well of course." Get in there Pugh.

"Yes, my eldest daughter has her mind firmly set on a

career on the stage. No shaking her I'm afraid. Perhaps you could give her a few acting lessons?"

Pugh blinked, bemused. "Acting lessons?"

"You said you were an actor."

"Did I?"

"You said you once did the same job as Albert Finney?"

When Pugh had explained that the job he had once shared with Albert Finney was the one in which the actor had machined a bicycle part the cycle manufacturer had lost all interest. Sadly the opportunity to offer his services to another cycle manufacturer had never presented itself again and Pugh had remained without a directorship to his name from that day to this.

He shook his head to rid his mind of what might have been, with a bit more luck, and reluctantly turned his thoughts to work. Not that he ever did much work; he let his three Junior Ministers, his Parliamentary Under Secretaries, do all the department's spadework. Why have a dog and bark yourself?

It was during the second of his previous two ministerial appointments, at Food and Agriculture, having had the experience of running Environment for eighteen months and making an utter balls of it, that it had dawned on Pugh that the best way to go about the business of being a Minister was to let his immediate subordinates make all the decisions. That way he could take credit for their actions when they got things right whilst firmly laying the blame at their door when they got things wrong. All he had to do was keep an eye on them.

At the moment the subordinates taking the decisions at the Department for Transport were Justin Dowell, responsible for the country's road and rail networks, Tony

Hilversum who looked after air transport and its constituent parts, and Ray Brick who looked after sea transport and everything else. Pugh couldn't abide any of them. He didn't like Dowell and Hilversum on principle, as both were champagne socialists, the spawn of Blair, the socialist equivalent of Hooray Henries, bloody nancy boys. Neither Dowell nor Hilversum had ever held down a proper job in their lives, the pair of them entering politics direct from university. In Pugh's unconsidered opinion, because it was something that didn't even need considering, if they'd had to live on their wits they would have died of starvation long ago.

He disliked Brick even more than he disliked Dowell and Hilversum. Although a Junior Minister Brick was older than Pugh by a few years, and like Pugh was one of the old school of socialists, a fire and brimstone man, a man who had been attracted to the Labour party and its ideals through its traditional connection with trade unionism. These credentials sat very well with Pugh. What didn't sit at all well with him was that Brick had his beady eyes on the Secretary for Transport's job, and to enhance his chances of achieving this ambition took every opportunity to show himself in good light, to the detriment of Pugh.

Brick's latest underhand move had been to wait until Pugh was out of the country on a two week fact-finding mission to The Bahamas before going behind his back to the Prime Minister with the solution to the long term coastguard problem. For this act of treason Pugh had tried to have Brick moved sideways to another Ministry, or even upwards to another Ministry but Phil, a close friend of Brick's son, an up-and-coming back-bencher and star of the future, would have none of it. Pugh hadn't pushed it in case he himself was moved sideways, or even worse downwards, perish the thought.

He contemplated his future yet again. What on earth could be done about it? Something would have to be, and pretty damn quick, that much was for certain.

CHAPTER TWO

A similarity Elton Arbuckle shared with Hugh Pugh was that for the first few years of his life he had liked his name. He liked it for its exclusivity. There were plenty of boys called Taylor or Smith or Jennings, but there was only one Arbuckle.

As was the case with Hugh Pugh he had begun to dislike it the day he started school, when his form teacher, twinkly old Miss Baker, with a warm smile and without a trace of malice, had called him 'Fatty'. Young boys were no less hurtful to their peers than in Hugh Pugh's childhood thirty years previously and Arbuckle's classmates had seized onto the nickname and called him Fatty for the rest of his schooldays. As Arbuckle was stick-thin he was at a loss as to understand why. One thing was certain though; he hadn't like being called Fatty, and had done his level best to discourage his classmates. But the more he protested the more they persisted, and from being the pleasant, well-adjusted five-year-old who had walked into Bessie Street Infants gaily swinging his little satchel he gradually turned into an introverted little boy who only ever swung his satchel after first aiming it at the head of one of his tormentors.

At the age of fourteen, whilst investigating his family tree on the internet, he had learned that the identity of the person whose nickname he now bore was the extremely fat Hollywood film star Roscoe Conkling 'Fatty' Arbuckle, a sex-mad fiend, who in an infamous case had been found guilty of rape. This caused him to retreat even further into his shell. It did carry a bonus with it however. Until then the young Arbuckle hadn't known what sex and rape were and had had to look up both words in his Oxford English Dictionary, one of his many school prizes. Having done so - and notwithstanding the shame brought down on him by his namesake - he had construed that sex must be something well worth having if someone had committed rape in order to get it. From that day on he had looked forward eagerly to the time he would have some of it for himself. Ten years later he was still looking forward to it.

If it was Arbuckle's introverted character which had caused him to cut himself off from the other boys, it was his classmates' treatment of him that was responsible for making him study much harder than they did, which gave him the determination to show them that although he might be known to them as Fatty it didn't stop him being a whole lot cleverer than they were. He had achieved this objective with flying colours. The cost was that it had made him into something of a loner, a trait he was to carry with him into adulthood.

Sadly, on leaving Bessie Street Infants at the age of eleven and transferring to the renowned Manchester Grammar School, the nickname 'Fatty' had accompanied him, thanks to the only other boy in his class with pretensions to cleverness switching to the same school. Thankfully, on completing his secondary education, he left the name Fatty behind him with the desks and blackboards. But by then it had shaped his future.

Thanks to his studies Arbuckle had become a very clever young man. Blessed with an I.Q. of 155 he could do the

Times crossword in an average time of nine minutes, he knew the answers to well over half the questions posed on *University Challenge* and he regularly outscored all four contestants in the general knowledge section of *Mastermind*. However he could never have held the Waterford Crystal trophy presented to the winner of *Mastermind* as he didn't have a specialist subject - although he knew quite a bit about most specialist subjects he was not sufficiently interested enough in any of them to explore them to *Mastermind* standard. Therefore at the age of eighteen he had fourteen GCSE 'A' levels and not the slightest idea of what to do with any of them, and when it came time to leave school for the university of his choice he not only didn't have a university of choice but even if he'd had one had no idea what he wished to study at it. What to do then?

He had done nothing. For ten years. His mornings were spent lying in bed, his afternoons and evenings doing whatever took his fancy. Fortunately his needs were few - the library, the internet, both free - and he found he could live comfortably, if not well, on the income support doled out by the state. The occasional luxury was made possible courtesy of hand-outs from his doting parents, both of whom were sure their gifted offspring would one day find his niche in life.

Arbuckle's only problem during this period of his life was that he wasn't getting any sex. Since he'd looked up the word he had spent many hours speculating about this mysterious coupling of the male and female bodies. He wondered what it was like. What it felt like. To put part of you into part of someone else. Did it hurt? Apparently it hurt the woman the first time but did it hurt the man too? It certainly hurt if you put your hard willy in the cardboard tube in the middle of a toilet roll, because in an effort to find out what sex felt like he'd tried that.

In his mission to find out more about sex he had turned to his good friend Google. The internet search engine had duly informed him where sex could be had, bought, watched, filmed, worshipped, discussed, successfully gone without (he ignored this as he was already expert at it), and simulated, but not what it was like.

One of the thousands of Google's pages on sex simulation had taken him to the weblog of Randy Andy, who had suggested that not only was a soapy roll a worthwhile alternative to sex but felt a lot like it too. Apparently the idea was to soap the hands thoroughly, then masturbate. A variation was to soap a sponge, wrap the sponge around the penis, then masturbate. Arbuckle tried both methods and although they had been all right he considered soapy rolls to be not all that much different than masturbating in the normal manner. However on the plus side he had ended up with a very clean penis. He certainly felt that actual sex must be a good deal better than a soapy roll or people wouldn't make such a fuss about it, they'd just settle for soapy rolls. Perhaps he should have used more soap? Or a different soap? He'd used Lifebuoy; would his mother's pink Camay be any better? He tried it, but apart from smelling nicer and attracting a funny look from the man who came to read the gas meter it had been no different, so he'd put soapy rolls on the back burner for the time being.

Sex with animals, cows and sheep especially, was claimed by several internet websites to be virtually the same as having sex with a woman. A Buxton smallholder preferred it. However cows and sheep were hard to come by in the Ardwick Green district of Manchester and the only animal Arbuckle ever came into regular contact with was next door's pit bull terrier. Fang was a bitch, but so is life sometimes, and the dog had once bitten him when he had encroached on its domain when retrieving his football. If the dog had bitten him just because he tried to get his ball back Arbuckle could only imagine what it might do to him if he tried to have intercourse with it, so this method of sexual fulfilment had joined soapy rolls on the back burner.

A third alternative, according to 'Meatblog' of Leeds, was Marmite. You either smeared it on your penis before jacking off or inserted as much of your penis as you could into the still full jar of Marmite then waggled the jar about. As this idea seemed to Arbuckle to be both a variation of the soapy roll and similar to his experiment with the toilet roll, but a whole lot messier, he hadn't seriously considered it, not even for the back burner. And it had put him off Marmite for life.

To get someone to have real sex with him was the answer, but this was easier said than done. This was partly because he was not an outgoing young man, blessed with the ability to charm, although even if he had been he would never have been able to afford to frequent the haunts - discos, clubs, gigs etc - where girls could be charmed. And partly because cultivating his high IQ and obtaining his fourteen GCSE's had necessitated his living a somewhat cloistered existence. In adulthood, as with many academics, this had resulted in his being hampered by a certain unworldliness, if not downright naiveté. Consequently, approaching his twenty-fourth birthday, he was still a virgin.

Since the age of seventeen, confident that his virginal state would not last for very much longer, he had carried a condom in his wallet. He had twice had to replace it, fearful that if and when the opportunity came to use it the rubber would have perished. Not wishing to waste his money completely he had masturbated in the first condom before throwing it away, but not in the second, as his experience with the first taught him that it was more enjoyable doing it without. He surmised from this that having sex whilst wearing a condom wouldn't be as enjoyable as sex without one and filed this in his mind for future reference.

Naturally he was aware that his chances of getting sex would improve if he had a regular girlfriend, but in nine years of trying he had only been able to get two: Rhoda, who turned out to be a lesbian, was even poorer than he was, and was only interested in him because she was an aficionado of the cinema and he paid for her to go; and Lola, whose name might have given him a clue, who turned out to be a transvestite. Again the cinema paid a part in Arbuckle's discovery of his potential conquest's true sexual leanings as it was on the back row of the local Odeon that he slipped his hand under Lola's skirt and put his hand not on the vagina he had been expecting to find there but on a throbbing hard on.

Wary of being ensnared by another Rhoda or Lola his natural insularity came to the fore and the only sexual experiences with women he'd had since had come courtesy of the previously mentioned five-fingered widow.

The niche his parents felt sure he would find one day presented itself the day after his twenty-third birthday in the shape of an advertisement in the *Daily Telegraph* (whose crossword he scorned as being too easy). Apparently Cleek University, a red-brick, ground-breaking, cutting-edge seat of learning (their description), was offering a degree course in 'Sex and Inflatable Rubber Woman Studies'. Its remit was 'To compare the differences between sex with a human female and sex with an inflatable rubber woman, with the object of promoting the latter as an alternative and safe means of sexual gratification'. The advert was designed to make young men like Arbuckle sit up and take notice. Arbuckle duly sat up and not only noticed but did so with great enthusiasm. At last a university was doing a course in something he was interested in. Sex. He was overjoyed, overcome, over the moon. On reading the rest of the advertisement, which went on to inform him that there was 'a shortage of experts in the sex and inflatable rubber woman field, whose skills would be in great demand as the sexual revolution gathered pace' he was over Venus, or whatever planet was sufficiently distant to match his euphoria; for as a man who had never had sex he found it difficult to see how he could spend three years at Cleek University comparing the differences between sex with a human female and sex with an inflatable rubber without having lots of it. He had applied to the university the same day and two weeks and a short interview later had been accepted.

The Department of Sex and Inflatable Rubber Woman Studies had been set up thanks to half the proceeds of a donation to Cleek University made by a generous benefactor. (The other half to go to the university to spend as they wished, a bribe for agreeing to host such a dodgy degree course as Sex and Inflatable Rubber Woman Studies in the first place). Elton Arbuckle was not aware of this of course. However he was to discover it later, to his great cost.

Arbuckle enjoyed university life. Unlike his school life nobody called him Fatty, although they might now have been justified in doing as due to his sedentary lifestyle over the last ten years he was about four stones overweight. He found the Sex and Inflatable Rubber Woman Studies course both interesting and disappointing; interesting in that it taught him many things about sex that he didn't know, disappointing in that after six months it still hadn't provided any of it.

He had expected that there would be female undergraduates on the course, who might be sympathetic to his longings, but disappointingly all ten of his fellow students turned out to be male. One of them, his next door neighbour Jeremy, who had switched from a ladies hairdressing degree course, had made it abundantly clear that he would more than welcome an advance from Arbuckle. Arbuckle however, although disappointed that he was still a virgin, wasn't yet ready to take the brown route to sexual gratification.

Rather than wait until the third year to embark on his thesis, as was the norm, Arbuckle had decided to make a start on it immediately, to do it at his leisure (and ultimately, he hoped, his pleasure). After just six months at Cleek he was more than halfway through his dissertation, to which he had given the rather ambitious working title 'All you ever wanted to know about inflatable rubber women but were afraid to ask', and was toying with the idea of presenting it to the university authorities at the end of his first year, thus saving himself the inconvenience of doing another two years at Cleek before setting himself up as a sex guru.

Which isn't to say that he wasn't enjoying university life. Far from it. He found being amongst people who were almost as clever as he, for the first time in his life, to be quite stimulating. The only dark cloud was that the students on the Sex and Inflatable Rubber Woman Studies course were looked upon by those reading more conventional subjects as being a bit weird, and this being the case the female students at Cleek University withheld their favours from them. As one of them had once succinctly put it to Arbuckle, when he had propositioned her: "Who wants to be studied while they're being shagged?"

So Arbuckle had continued to labour at his undergraduate studies under that constraint. However he was confident it wouldn't be too long before he finally popped his cherry.

CHAPTER THREE

Rap...rap...rap! Henry Willoughby rapped the dildo three times on the table top to call the weekly meeting to order.

Various local groups used the large, high-vaulted upstairs meeting room of *The Grim Jogger* public house in south Derby. Tonight, Friday, it was the turn of VAST, Vigilantes Against Sex Toys, to hold court. Present at the meeting were eight of the nine members of VAST, Mr Willoughby, Mr Grimshaw, Mr Seal, Father Flannery, Mr Khan, Councillor Mrs Wisbech JP, Mrs Bean and Miss Preece. Plus initially, until he found out his mistake, a member of the Orienteering Club who had managed to find his way there but on the wrong night. Willoughby had welcomed him and offered him membership but he had declined, saying that if people wanted to use sex toys it was their own business. Willoughby told him in no uncertain manner that it was also the business of VAST, and very much so.

When Willoughby had rapped the dildo on the table top Emily Preece, spinster of this parish, had visibly blanched. "I really wish you wouldn't do that, Mr Willoughby," she reproved him.

Willoughby treated her to an apologetic smile but the tone of his voice indicated that he would not be swayed. "I do need to call the meeting to order Miss Preece."

"Not with that thing you don't. You could use a gavel, like any normal chairman, or rap on the desk with a coin or your knuckles, or just simply say 'I call the meeting to order'."

Willoughby sighed. Miss Preece hadn't been a member for long and perhaps hadn't yet grasped the full significance of the dildo. He reminded her. "It's ceremonial, Emily. The very first ever sex toy we persuaded a member of the public to give up. It serves to remind us of why we are here."

"I don't need reminding why I'm here, I know exactly why I'm here, I'm reminded of it every time I pass the sex shop in the High Street," said Miss Preece, from atop her high horse. She pointed at the dildo. "There's one of those....things in the window this week."

"Well it is by no means unusual for a shop to put its wares in the window. And much as we would like to stop them including dildos in their display I'm afraid there isn't a lot we can do about it. However, like I say, our dildo is merely symbolic."

"It is diabolic."

And to Emily Preece it was diabolic. In her eyes dildos were something the Devil himself might have invented. As a member of VAST she was naturally against all sex toys in any shape or form, but especially in the shape and form of artificial penises.

In fact it was a dildo that had been instrumental in her joining the group, some six months earlier. A girls' school teacher of English Language and Literature, she had been asked by the headmistress to oversee a training session of the sixth form 4 x 100 metres relay team - the games mistress having been forced to make an emergency visit to the dentist. Having little time for sport Miss Preece had been far more interested in a re-visitation of the carryings on of Elizabeth Bennet and Mr D'Arcy in her new edition of *Pride and Prejudice* than she was with her charges. Consequently, with only half an eye on them, she had failed to detect what the girls were using as a baton. The half an eye she did have on them had noticed, for reasons she couldn't discern, that Caroline

Durant, who was running the second leg, seemed very reluctant to pass the baton on to Sharon Pengelli, who was running the third leg. More often than not they failed to exchange it at all, both girls collapsing in fits of laughter before this seemingly simple task could be achieved. It wasn't until she wandered over to the girls, whilst they were seated on the ground taking five, and saw it nestling between Caroline's thighs, business end pointed towards her crotch, that she realised what it was.

"Is....is that thing what I think it is?" she said, blushing violently.

"Why what do you think it is, Miss?" said Caroline, artfully.

"Isn't it a baton, Miss Preece?" asked Sharon, like her friend not one to miss the opportunity of having a bit of fun at the expense of their prudish English teacher.

Miss Preece, refusing to be drawn, had taken the dildo gingerly between finger and thumb, and with some difficulty, as it was a dildo of generous proportions, put it in her handbag. Having dismissed the girls and ordered them to take a cold shower she took the offending apparatus to the headmistress, Mrs Jones.

"Look what I found the relay team using as a baton," she said, turning her handbag upside down and letting the dildo drop onto Mrs Jones's desk with a loud 'thunk'.

"Oh dear," said Mrs Jones.

"Oh dear, indeed. How on earth would the girls come by such a thing?

If it had been any of her staff other than Miss Preece who had presented such a double entendre Mrs Jones might have cashed in on it and shared a laugh with them. Instead she gave a rueful smile. "Unfortunately in the times in which we live they are generally available, Emily; and that being the case I'm afraid they are bound to fall into innocent young hands occasionally."

"Well they won't be falling into innocent young hands any longer. Not if I have anything to do with it," stormed Miss Preece, and, although not entirely convinced that the young hands the dildo had fallen into were completely innocent, had from that point on made every effort to make her words come true.

She had achieved only limited success. One small victory had been a successful objection to the opening of a sex shop in an old Methodist chapel which now served the community as a bingo hall - despite strong opposition from the Methodists, who had originally objected to their church becoming a bingo hall and would have preferred it to become a sex shop. However her campaign had bought her to the attention of VAST, who at the time were also objecting to the proposed sex shop. Willoughby had invited Miss Preece to join them and Miss Preece, adopting the maxim of strength in numbers, had abandoned her solo efforts and joined forces with them.

It was the use of the dildo as a sort of ceremonial gavel that sometimes made her wish she hadn't. However, that apart, she was aware that her being a member of VAST was more likely to rid the world of sex toys than if she had remained a lone campaigner.

"Before we move on to tonight's agenda there is one apology for absence," said Mr Willoughby. "From Mr Cleaver."

"And he has much to apologise for," chimed in Constance Wisbech.

"Why, what has he done?" George Grimshaw had missed

the last meeting, when it had been reported that Mr Cleaver had set fire to a branch of the Body Shop, an act of arson that had given the local fire brigade an unwelcome afternoon out.

Mrs Wisbech filled him in as to Mr Cleaver's transgression.

"Why did he do that?" asked Arthur Seal, who had also missed the last meeting as it clashed with a darts match. "What has he got against Body Shops?"

"Nothing. He mistook it for an Ann Summers shop. Apparently there was a naked mannequin lying down in the shop window awaiting the attention of the window dresser," explained Willoughby, "and the shop's cat had taken the liberty of taking forty winks on its lap. Mr Cleaver thought it was some sort of grotesque sex toy, and...." he spread his hands in a hopeless gesture and left the rest of the sentence unsaid.

"And what is his reason, other than his bizarre behaviour, for tendering his apologies?" said Miss Preece.

"He is indisposed."

"He is in prison," said Mrs Wisbech, in a manner which left no one in any doubt that she thought it was no less than Cleaver deserved. "For twenty eight days. I myself was instrumental in sending him there. He has another two weeks to serve, unless he is released for good behaviour; which is highly unlikely if his past behaviour is anything to go by."

"Why, has he got previous?" said Seal, lapsing into the vernacular of the police officer he had been before recently retiring from the force.

"I meant burning the Body Shop down. People of that ilk don't deserve to be a member of VAST."

Mrs Bean, aka Brown Owl, tried to introduce an element of reason into the discussion "We all have a right to be against the evil of sex toys, Mrs Wisbech," she said.

"Even the fallen," agreed one of VAST's founder members, Father Fergus Flannery.

"I am entitled to my opinion," said Mrs Wisbech. "And I stand by it. The man is a thoroughly bad lot; it wasn't the first time he'd been up before me."

"Anyway he's sent his apologies," said Willoughby, anxious to move on. He looked around at the other seven of the eight members of VAST present that evening. "Now are there any matters arising from last month's meeting?" Mrs Wisbech raised a hand. "Yes, Madam Honorary Secretary?"

Mrs Wisbech got to her feet. Holding a letter as though it were contaminated she regarded it with as much distaste as she could muster, which was quite considerable; registering distaste came easy to her as she lived next door to a financial adviser.

Mrs Wisbech was responsible for penning and signing the organisation's letters of complaint, Willoughby being of the opinion that the Justice of the Peace initials behind her name added more weight to their missives. It was apparent from her demeanour and tone of voice that whatever weight may have been added on this occasion hadn't been enough to influence the writer of the letter now in her hand. She cleared her throat and spoke. "As agreed in committee I wrote to the owners of the former barber's shop in Belper, which is now polluting the town as a sex shop. I pointed out to them that the barber's pole still remained in position from the property's previous use, and that as long as it remained there members of the public might be misled into construing that it was doing service as a phallic symbol, and would they therefore kindly remove it. I have their reply here." She read from the letter. "'*Dear Madam, Thank you for your letter of the*

20th inst. We hadn't realised the barber's pole was still there and will be painting it pink'." She scowled. "No less than can be expected from the sort people who run sex shops, I suppose. Although I shall be writing to them again of course, and in much stronger terms."

"Of course, Mrs Wisbech." Willoughby thought she might be wasting her time but refrained from saying so in case a protracted discussion developed; there were more important things to discuss that evening. He quickly moved on. "The first item on the agenda is our annual trip to the Sex Toys Exhibition, which will be held this year in Blackpool."

"Oh goody," said Mrs Bean, clapping her hands together in delight, "I'll be able to have a ride on The Big One. I had a ride on it last year when I took a party of Guides and Brownies; we all found it quite exhilarating." She frowned as she recalled the experience. "Although it did make two of the younger Brownies quite bilious."

Willoughby, his mind still on phalluses and the Sex Toys Exhibition thought for one horrible moment that Mrs Bean was referring to some monstrous new example of the most basic of aids to female sexual satisfaction before realising she was talking about Blackpool's giant roller coaster. He breathed a sigh of relief.

Miss Preece was puzzled. "Why would we want to go to an exhibition of sex toys?"

Willoughby was on firmer ground here. "Of course being a fairly new member you wouldn't know, Miss Preece. You see we are in the habit of going every year in order to keep abreast..." He stopped and searched for another word, feeling that abreast, although not an incorrect word, was perhaps not a suitable one for the chairman of VAST to be using. "Er.... in order to keep tabs on, the latest products in the sex toys industry."

"To keep tabs on them?"

"Specifically to take note of any new items which may have been introduced during the last twelve months and will no doubt be finding their way onto the shelves of the establishments who trade in such filth."

"I would have thought we would be seeing them quite soon enough when they hit the shelves," said Miss Preece loftily.

"That's the problem I'm afraid, they don't all hit the shelves. Many of them are sold under the counter."

The schoolteacher was surprised on learning this. "Even in this day and age?"

"Especially in this day and age. Not all frequenters of sex shops are happy to see things like......pardon my French.....Donkey Dicks on open sale."

"And self-circumcision kits," said Grimshaw.

"And self-circumcision kits."

"And Prince Charles butt plugs."

"What on earth is a butt plug?" said Mrs Wisbech.

"I believe it's a plastic or rubber device that homosexuals push up their rectums for the purposes of pleasure," said Willoughby uncomfortably.

"And a Prince Charles butt plug specifically?" asked Mrs Wisbech, although as a staunch monarchist not really wishing to know the answer.

"A butt plug moulded in the image of the head of the Prince of Wales," explained Willoughby. "Apparently the ears make for added sensitivity."

"Cupid's Four Finger Tingler," said Grimshaw, continuing the list of things that some frequenters of sex shops might not be happy to see on open sale.

"Yes all right, Mr Grimshaw, I think we've made our point," said Willoughby. He paused before going on. "I will put us all down for the visit to the Sex Toys Exhibition then? And our usual fish and chip supper afterwards, of course." There were no dissenters although Miss Preece looked very dubious about it all. "Excellent." He referred to the sheet of A4 in front of him. "So then, the second item on the agenda is funding. I'm afraid the purchase of the portable X-ray machine, now being used to excellent effect by Mr Grimshaw, has depleted our funds quite considerably. Consequently we need to get them up to a healthy level again." He looked around the members. "Has anyone had any ideas as to how we might boost our coffers?"

"I was thinking a flag day perhaps," said Fr Flannery.

"I'm pretty sure you have to be a registered charity to hold a flag day," warned Mrs Wisbech, the club's legal brain. "Like lifeboats."

"Then a registered charity we shall become. After all we are just as essential as lifeboats, are we not. Indeed we are not dissimilar to them, taking as we do to the troubled waters to save the souls of those unfortunates wallowing in their murky depths," said Flannery, sounding as though he were delivering one of his Sunday sermons, but to a possibly larger congregation.

"You could well be right," said Grimshaw, "But given the choice I think a man drowning at sea would welcome the sight of an approaching lifeboat a bit more than us pitching up and trying to talk him out of using a French Tickler," he continued, demonstrating his knowledge of both human nature and available sex toys.

"Perhaps someone could look into the possibilities?" said Willoughby. "Perhaps...."

"Why we need raise money anyway?"

As one, the other members of VAST turned to Farzad Khan, the man whose interjection had interrupted Willoughby. Up until now Khan had spent the entire meeting sat slightly apart from the others, brooding. He was exceptionally good at brooding and often spent the whole meeting doing it, never once saying a word.

Before Khan had finally been accepted as a member of Vigilantes Against Sex Toys there had been grave reservations expressed by the members. And there had been even graver reservations ever since, the main one being that whilst they had nothing against Afghans *per se*, Khan not only looked very Afghan but exacerbated it by dressing like one. His normal attire was a loose black and grey striped dress-like garment, a sheepskin waistcoat, a turban, voluminous trousers and knee boots. If this wasn't bad enough, in place of his missing right hand he had a hook, which coupled with his permanently bloodshot eyes and his long flowing beard gave him a quite fearsome appearance. His nose, permanently scarred and habitually bloodied through his occasional habit of unconsciously picking his nose with his hook, didn't improve matters.

Problems had been foreseen. The members of VAST, like Jehovah's Witnesses, operated in pairs when they doorstepped people, and while it was one thing for two of them to enter a sex shop and politely argue with its owner that it was morally wrong for him to be plying his trade, and would he therefore kindly desist, it was quite another for one of them to do it whilst accompanied by someone who looked like a Taliban terrorist. Grimshaw had ventured the opinion that this might be no bad thing, since a sex shop owner confronted by a bloodied Afghan with a hook might be more likely to accede to their request to shut up shop. Willoughby however had pointed out that although this was probably true, Vigilantes Against Sex Toys was and always would be a strictly non-violent organisation.

A further complication was that Khan, on detecting that the members of VAST were not exactly falling over themselves to accept him, had begun to issue dark mutterings on the subject of racial discrimination. With this hanging over their heads, and the possible repercussions it might bring with it, it had finally been decided to accept Khan as a member, with the provision that when he accompanied one of the other members to a sex shop he dispensed with his headwear, wore a suit and covered up his hook. Khan had agreed, although with some reluctance, and was duly elected. However all the members were well aware that a close eye would have to be kept on the Afghan, and with good reason, as he had exhibited increasingly militant tendencies of late. For example instead of writing to the owner of the sex shop that was formerly a barber shop he had advocated eschewing a letter altogether and going round there and snapping off his pole.

When addressing Khan Willoughby always took care to apply a conciliatory tone to his voice, ever-mindful of the Afghan's hook and the damage it might wreak if its owner suddenly went berserk. He did this now, in reply to Khan's questions as to why the society needed funds. "Well for all manner of things, Mr Khan," he said. "The hire of this room for example. Our visits to far flung sex shops. Stationery and stamps so that we may write to these sex shops in an attempt to get them to...."

Khan exploded. "Bah! Write to them? What is point? They laugh at our letters. I piss on them. We should go to them, demand they stop their filthy doings!" He raised his hook high in the hair. A glint of light reflected on it, making the implement look even more fearsome than it already was. "If had this through their jocular would not be laughing at us."

"Their jocular?" said Mrs Wisbech, wondering what part of the anatomy a jocular was.

"Their jocular, their jocular, their jocular vein!" screamed Khan impatiently, pointing the hook at his throat.

Mr Willoughby had no doubt that if sex shop proprietors had Khan's hook through their jugular vein they would not only fail to laugh at them but would probably be incapable of ever laughing again, and a good thing too, but felt constrained to point out to the Afghan that, as effective as this course of action might be, it was not the way forward.

"Well should be way forward," said Khan. "We sit here chewing fats and footypussing around while wife and children dare not look in shop window in case it have disgusting sex toy in it."

Mrs Wisbech stepped in. "We share your concerns of course, Mr Khan, but in this country there is a way we go about doing things."

"Yes. Footypussing way."

"The word is pussyfooting actually, Mr Khan," advised Miss Preece.

"Pussyfooting, footypussing, fuckingpussy, make no difference what you call it. While all time filthy sex toys like Wankee-Doodle-Dandy offend followers of Allah!"

"Like what?" said Mr Grimshaw.

"It's something new from America apparently," said Willoughby. "Mr Khan brought it in. He showed it to me before the rest of you arrived."

"My children they play with it!" said Khan, his eyes

burning like hot coals. "I find them playing with Wankee-Doodle-Dandy, find on rubbish council tip."

"What exactly is a Wankee-Doodle-Dandy?" asked Miss Preece. "I've heard of a Yankee-Doodle-Dandy."

"Apparently it's a sort of male masturbation apparatus," said Willoughby. "The male equivalent of a vibrator."

"Not same as vibrator. Eldest son Atash not able get hand stuck in vibrator, able get hand stuck in Wankee-Doodle-Dandy. Did get hand stuck in Wankee-Doodle-Dandy. Can not wipe bottom properly now, damage bottom-wiping hand."

"Can't he use his other hand?" said Mr Seal, helpfully.

"Not possible. One hand for eating, other hand for wiping shitty bottom. Not use hand that wipe shitty bottom to eat with, not use hand to eat with to wipe shitty bottom."

Mrs Bean pulled a face. "Please, Mr Khan, too much information."

Fr Flannery was about to ask Khan which hand he used to wipe his bottom with, feeling that it might be a bit dodgy if his religion dictated he had to wipe it with the hand that had been replaced by a hook, and if that was the case would he consider converting to Catholicism to alleviate the problem, but the Afghan had already returned to his theme. "Too much footypussing," said Khan. "Why we call Vigilantes Against Sex Toys? We not vigilantes. If was vigilantes would be going for their joculars."

"Being vigilantes doesn't imply that we should go for their joculars....jugulars, Mr Khan. "We are vigilantes only in the sense that we are self-appointed guardians of the public's morals."

"Footypussing."

"Not at all."

"I piss on you."

"Now steady on Mr Khan, there's no need for that sort of talk," scolded Willoughby.

Khan fell silent and returned to his brooding. Willoughby sighed. There was trouble ahead he was sure.

CHAPTER FOUR

As a wine connoisseur Pugh could never inhale his own excrement without being reminded that a leading wine merchant, Alastair Hanson of Haynes, Hanson and Clark if his memory served him correctly, had once remarked that very good burgundy smelled of shit. Pugh had never found conclusive evidence of Hanson's contention but could vouch wholeheartedly for its veracity if the burgundy was included in a melange of fine French cuisine.

He was reminded of this as he took a moment off from another day of worrying about his dire situation, leaned to one side, lifted a buttock an inch or so off his chair and farted. There was no one else in the room so it didn't matter, and even if there had been it still didn't matter, he was the Secretary of State for Transport and if the Secretary of State for Transport couldn't fart in his own office then who could? The embossed wallpaper and thick carpets would quickly absorb it anyway. He'd maybe have to open a window.

The room was instantly perfumed with the aroma of what pate de fois gras, langoustine a la crème au gratin and Nuits Saint Georges smelt like after it had fought its way through his overworked digestive tract and marinated and matured in his bowels overnight. Pugh inhaled. The smell was disgusting. He knew it would be even more disgusting for someone else, other people's farts always smelled worse than your own, and imagined how nice it would be if one of his Junior Ministers was to pop by and get a good whiff of his latest creation. Wishful thinking; none of his immediate subordinates would dare to drop into his office unbidden. On a couple of occasions he had ordered them to come, and had conjured up a fart on demand, but he had to be in a playful mood to do that sort of thing and today his mood, with all his worries bearing down on him, was quite the opposite of playful.

The single sheet of paper, placed there by Myra a few minutes ago on his empty Sherwood Forest desk, informed him that he had only one appointment that day, a lunchtime meeting with a delegation of government officials and transport consultants from Sierra Leone. Did they have transport in Sierra Leone, he wondered? Apart from elephants? Where exactly was Sierra Leone anyway? Africa, wasn't it? Probably, it sounded African. But Sierra sounded a bit South American too - *The Treasure of the Sierra Madre*, that film with Humphrey Bogart, that was in South America, and they'd gone around on horses and donkeys in that when they weren't squabbling over gold. He'd have to ask Myra before the delegation arrived; all the members of the delegation would be able to speak at least a bit of English if they were anything like the usual darkies who came a lot more often than they were welcome, but he didn't want to risk making a fool of himself by asking them about the current situation *vis a vis* their elephants if they rode about on donkeys. He flicked down the switch on his inter-com. "Get me everything we have on transport in the Sierra Madre, Myra."

"The Sierra Madre, Minister?"

"Where that delegation I'm lunching with come from."

She corrected him. "Sierra Leone."

"That's the place. It is in Africa is it?"

"It was the last time I looked, Minister."

Pugh raised his eyebrows on hearing his secretary's final sentence. Had he detected a slightly mocking tone in her voice? Was it possible she was being sarcastic? Could it be that as she was aware he would soon be out through the door and a new man ensconced in his seat that it was making her a little disrespectful? Because she'd never shown him any disrespect before. Not once. It had always been Minister this Minister that Minister the other since day one. Myra was far better educated than he was, he knew that, but never at any time in the past had she shown this, never been in the slightest bit uppity about it. But that was then and this is now, and now was when he would very soon be out on his ear. He resolved to monitor the situation; the last thing he wanted on top off all his other problems was subordinates showing him disrespect.

Of course it could simply be that Sierra Leone used to be in Africa but wasn't there anymore. There could have been a border change following a war, they were always fighting each other over there when they weren't fucking each other; maybe that was what Myra had meant when she'd said it was in Africa the last time she'd looked? Countries were always changing their borders nowadays, and their names, Sri Lanka, Bejing, Mumbai and all that rubbish.

Whilst waiting for Myra to come up with the goods Pugh began to wonder what it was like in Sierra Leone, what it was like under its African or South American skies. Better than the shithole that was England in a wet January, that was for sure. But was it worthy of a fact-finding mission? What were the beaches like over there and the booze and the nosh and the nightlife and the availability and quality of legover? The weather would be hot, whether it was in Africa or South America, definitely. Could it perhaps be a more desirable destination than The Maldives, which he had earmarked as the next country deserving of a fact-finding mission? And would be leaving for in the not too distant future.

Regarding The Maldives, he didn't know if there were any facts to find there, or even if it had a transport system to find facts about, but more importantly what he did know was that it was looked upon by those Members of Parliament who had visited it as a very rewarding location in which to spend a couple of weeks.

It was almost six months since he'd been on his last fact-finding mission so another one was well overdue; his jollies were not normally spaced so far apart. Why had he left it so long? Then he remembered why so much time had passed since his last excursion at the expense of the British tax payer. It was because the bastard newspapers had kicked off about it and made his life a bloody misery when they'd found out he'd taken his girlfriend Lorelei along with him as his '*secretary*' (the newspapers' quotation marks). Naturally he had claimed that Lorelei was indeed his secretary and a fully qualified and extremely efficient one at that, but a telephone call to her by one of the red tops asking her if she used Pitman, Gregg or Teeline and Lorelei's reply of "Whassaat?" had indicated otherwise.

Pugh sighed yet again. Six months without a jolly! If a week is a long time in politics surely six months should be plenty of time for the press to forgive and forget, but would it have? Not if he knew it. Fleet Street could be like a dog with a bone when it wanted to be, and after Loreleigate, which one newspaper had wittily named it, he didn't fancy being the bone again.

He would have to go on a fact-finding mission soon though, press or no press, he really needed a break, some time to himself, time away from it all, time to think out his future. He wouldn't be able to take Lorelei though, otherwise the media would go berserk. She wouldn't like being left behind in the cold of an English winter while he was living it up in The Maldives, or possibly Sierra Leone, but if it meant the difference between him soaking up the sun for a couple of weeks or not soaking it up she would just have to lump it.

He knew that what he really needed, what he needed more than anything, even more than another jolly, was a good idea. An idea that would make him some money, so that it wouldn't really matter when the time came that the axe fell and he lost his job and his living along with it. Not a fortune – although a fortune would do very nicely thank you – but enough to live on in the manner to which he had become accustomed. An idea like the one the bloke who invented that revolutionary vacuum cleaner had come up with....what was he called now? Tyson.... Dyson.... Mike Dyson, that was him. Mike Dyson, lucky old, jammy old Mike Dyson. Or that Yank, Colonel Sanders, the lucky bugger who invented that Kentucky Fried Chicken shite with the secret recipe. An idea like that. A good idea that would make him a mint. It needn't be an idea for something useful like a vacuum cleaner either; an idea similar to the one the bloke whose idea it had been to persuade people to walk along dragging a Nordic Pole in each hand would do just as well.

Pugh couldn't think about the Nordic Pole phenomenon without wondering all over again at the bizarreness and sheer unlikelihood of it all. It was truly amazing; people had been walking around unaided quite happily for hundreds of years then somebody comes along and persuades them they need a couple of fancy pointed sticks, at anything from a tenner to fifty quid a throw, to enable them to put one leg in front of the other, and makes a bloody fortune out of them doing it. Lucky bastard.

A good idea in a growth industry was what he wanted. Cancer; that was a 'growth' industry. He smiled to himself at his thought, happy in the knowledge that even in adversity he had still managed to retain his sense of humour. But what were the growth industries in Great Britain nowadays. Assuming there were any left? There weren't any in manufacturing. Cars, engineering, steel, they were all either gone or in the ownership of foreigners; the Krauts, the Japs, the Yanks, even the Spanish for God's sake.

Not alcohol or tobacco either. Apart from a privileged few only the young could afford to drink much in the way of alcohol these days. And as far as smoking went fewer and fewer people than ever were doing it and the Government was doing its level best to ensure that the few who did smoke did it even less. Though God knows where they would get the money from that they currently got from the tax on tobacco if they ever succeeded in stopping it altogether. The dim buggers hadn't thought about that. Probably alcohol if anybody was still drinking it by then.

Or the sex industry. Now that *was* a growth industry, you'd only got to look at the small ads in any newspaper; prostitution, sex toys, blow-up dolls, phone sex, you name it you could get it, and more of it than you ever could before. He thought about it for a moment. Yes, a good idea in the sex industry would be ideal. But then there would be Phil to contend with, prissy Phil and all the fuss he'd created when he'd found out about the mobile massage parlour, so best look somewhere else for a good idea.

An idea suddenly struck him from completely out of the blue. Not a good idea, not the good idea he was searching so desperately for, but an idea that might lead him to having a good idea. If he couldn't come up with something of his own maybe he could merge other people's good ideas to form a new idea of his own? He chewed on it a little, gave it a coat of looking at. A Nordic vacuum cleaner perhaps? Sort of a Hoover Constellation type thing with a pair of horns sticking out of the top of it, like a Viking helmet? A sort of novelty hoover. It would be popular with the Nordics, but did Nordics have carpets to hoover, they all had wooden floors over there didn't they? He was sure they'd all had wooden floors when he'd gone there on that fact-finding mission to Amsterdam, when he'd been at Environment. Nordic Fried Chicken, perhaps? Kentucky Fried Nordic Poles? Kentucky Fried Hoovers? "Kentucky Fried arseholes," he spat out, losing whatever was left of his temper on recognising he was going up yet another blind alley.

The Secretary of State for Transport had spent many hours sat in his office with his head in his hands trying to come up with a good idea but had yet to come up with an even half good idea. On one occasion he thought he'd had a good idea, when he came up with the notion of the mobile massage parlour, which he'd imagined at the time would be a racing certainty to succeed. The idea had arrived, as welcome as it had been unexpected, whilst he'd been spending a weekend in his double-flipped country cottage in his Derbyshire constituency.

The circumstances that provoked the idea were fortuitous. A mobile hairdresser had called on Lorelei to titivate her hair prior to an evening at the pub and whilst waiting for her he had turned on the TV. He hadn't expected to find anything worth watching on his high definition set from amongst the low definition programmes the television companies offer up as entertainment on Saturday evenings, so was pleasantly surprised when his channel hopping dropped him off in the middle of a documentary about dodgy massage parlours. An hour later when they were walking down to the pub, and with the dodgy massage parlours still fresh in his mind, they had passed a mobile blacksmith shoeing a horse in the drive of a large house. "Look at that, a mobile blacksmith!" Lorelei had exclaimed. "Whatever next?" And immediately, wonderfully, Pugh had known what next. A mobile massage parlour. For surely such an enterprise would be a welcome attraction for a businessman desirous of a bit of hanky panky, but too tired from a day at the office to make the journey into town? Surely such a service would be popular with another businessman, similarly desirous of hanky panky, but who might be afraid to venture into an area where hanky panky could be had in case someone saw him and shopped him to his better half?

Plans were drawn up immediately. A feasibility study carried out. Using his contacts Pugh acquired, gratis, a large van that had recently been retired from service as a Derbyshire County Council mobile library. Using fond memory he then acquired one Lucy Lambert to provide the massage and extra services which the mobile massage parlour would provide. The inside of the van was stripped of its pine bookcases and fitted out as a massage parlour; the walls were decorated with expensive wallpaper, the floor was covered with a carpet even more expensive than the one Pugh had in his office, soft lights were added, sweet music, exotically perfumed unguents, sex aids, the lot. All claimed as necessary Parliamentary expenses of course.

The first appointment was secured, a Mr Stokes of Hampstead. In what he imagined to be a stroke of genius Pugh had kept the outside of the van exactly as it was, with the words Derbyshire County Council Public Library Service in large letters on both sides. His reasoning was that a client's wife, on seeing a van with Mobile Massage Parlour emblazoned on it when it drew up outside the family home, might view such a vehicle with suspicion. Especially if shortly after its arrival her husband disappeared inside it for half-an-hour and came out of it not refreshed and raring to go but absolutely knackered and fit for nothing. Even if the van were plain it still might be regarded by a wife as being more than a little unusual on observing her spouse clamber eagerly into the back of it with an expectant look on his face. However it was unlikely in the extreme that it would be looked upon as suspicious if a client happened to look out of his front window, nodded towards the van and told his wife he was just popping out to the library to change his book.

Unfortunately the scheme had hit a major hitch at the very first hurdle when Mrs Frost, the Stokes's next-door-neighbour, saw the van parked outside and went in to change her library books at the same time Lucy Lambert was giving Mr Stokes a blow job.

Naturally not wishing another such occurrence Pugh had put on his thinking cap and come up with the idea of disguising the true purpose of the massage parlour by painting out the words 'Derbyshire County Council Public Library Service' and substituting them with the words 'Mobile Garden Centre'. Underneath he had added 'By Appointment Only', in order to keep out anyone who failed to make the necessary booking. This had worked well for a couple of days and might still be doing well today had not the Deputy Head of the Scotland Yard Vice Squad called in to make an appointment to purchase a selection of wallflowers and wisteria and discovered that the only things on offer that night were a tone-up and a wank.

A quiet but firm word of warning from the senior police officer sadly put an end to Pugh's ambitions in the mobile massage parlour business.

Myra now came in with the information on all things Sierra Leone. Apparently it was definitely in Africa so he decided that the fact-finding mission would be to The Maldives. Africans were all right, especially when it came to grabbing himself a piece of black velvet, but one could have too much of them, and there was certainly too much of them in Africa; he'd found that out on a fact-finding mission to Kenya, you couldn't move for the buggers, and if they weren't singing and dancing they were banging a drum.

Myra also brought in the morning's external mail with her. Apart from one letter marked 'Private and Confidential' all the letters had been opened and relevant parts of the text highlighted by Pugh's Parliamentary Under Secretary for the Minister's information.

Having delivered the mail Myra left Pugh to his deliberations, the first of which was to ogle her bottom on her way out, something he found quite impossible to resist. It was quite natural for him, almost a reflex action. He did the same when any young woman presented him with a view of her bottom, he couldn't help himself.

He would have loved to have propositioned Myra, an attractive-looking thirty-year-old with a good figure that was never completely disguised by the severely tailored business suits she always wore to the office, would have loved to take her to bed. But he never had and never would as he made a point of never sleeping with a woman who was more intelligent than he was, a constraint that limited the supply of possible conquests far more than he imagined.

Pugh's appetite for what women could provide him with

was as healthy as his appetite for food and drink. He had once wondered whether he was over-sexed compared to other men but after due consideration had decided he wasn't. Leastways not when compared to his fellow Members of Parliament, the majority of whom would shag a kangaroo if they could stop it hopping. He conceded however that he might be over-sexed when compared to ordinary men.

He now applied himself to the task of dealing with the external mail. He'd dealt with the pile of internal mail dumped unceremoniously on his desk by Myra an hour earlier by gazing at it disinterestedly for a couple of minutes before throwing the lot in the bin. None of the letters would have contained anything he needed to know. There hadn't been a question on transport tabled for that day, which he would have had to answer in the Commons, so it would all be shite, and he had enough shite to deal with as it was.

He now gave the same treatment to the pile of external mail as he'd given to the internal mail. But fortunately not before removing the unopened letter marked 'Private and Confidential'. For it was the contents of this letter that indirectly led to Pugh having the good idea for which he craved. And possibly his salvation.

CHAPTER FIVE

"When did you first decide to have sex with an inflatable rubber woman?"

"When I realised I was never going to get sex with a real woman."

"You weren't prepared to wait any longer?"

"How long am I supposed to wait? I'm nearly forty for Christ's sake."

"You never had a girlfriend?"

"Not one who would let me have it off with her."

"You could have paid for sex. You could have gone to a prostitute."

"I don't pay for sex."

"You paid for the inflatable rubber woman."

"That's different."

"I don't see the distinction; money left your pocket in exchange for sex."

"Oh fuck this for a game of soldiers!"

Arbuckle got up from the only chair in his student flat and stopped the tape on the mobile recorder. Not much he could use there. Nothing in fact. Just the usual stuff from yet another sad bastard who did it with inflatable rubber women because he couldn't find a woman who would accommodate him. Precisely the same reason given by eighty two per cent of all the other men he'd interviewed.

It was the other eighteen per cent he was interested in. The ones who had sex solely with inflatable rubber women. The ones who still had sex with inflatable rubber women even though they could get it with a real woman. The ones who expressed a definite preference for having it with inflatable rubber women; who would rather have it with an inflatable rubber woman than with a real woman. The ones who didn't even like inflatable rubber women but absolutely loved rubber. The one's who liked to have it with inflatable rubber women while their wives were watching. (How the wives felt about this, whether they were offended or whether they were just thankful it wasn't their husband banging away brainlessly and breathlessly at them yet again, he couldn't guess and they couldn't say.)

He would soon be finding out how one such woman felt about it, however. The Sex and Inflatable Rubber Woman Studies Department had learned via the *Loose Women* television show's publicity department that one of the subjects up for discussion on the day's agenda would be about inflatable rubber women. Apparently a distressed female viewer had written in to say she was forced to share the marital bed with one. Arbuckle and his co-students had been advised by their tutor that in being questioned about this unhappy state of affairs the woman might reveal something which may help them with the Inflatable Rubber Woman (Opposition and Objections to) module of their coursework.

As he stopped the tape he wondered how many interviews he had done thus far? How many would he need? You could go on indefinitely but after a while you kept getting the same answers, you reached saturation point. He hadn't had a new answer for a fortnight so what was the point in doing any more? Maybe he'd give it another ten interviews or so and then see. In the meantime it was about time he himself had sex with an inflatable rubber woman, he'd been putting it off for long enough. He'd have a cup of tea first though, take a break.

Ten minutes later he drained his cup of Earl Grey (a tea blend with a distinctive flavour and aroma derived from the addition of oil extracted from the rind of the bergamot orange, named after the 2nd Earl Grey, British Prime Minister the 1830s, eat your hearts out *Mastermind* contestants) and glanced at his watch. Almost one-o-clock. He switched on his TV set for *Loose Women* and turned his attention to the inflatable rubber woman from An Hour In Bed which had arrived by post that morning.

Unfortunately the university did not stretch to providing sex dolls with which their students might enjoy intercourse so Arbuckle had been forced to provide his own. When he'd logged on to the internet to browse through the vast selection available he had found many examples that were more attractive than Bouncy Beyoncé, the one he had finally plumped for. In fact some of those on offer were more attractive-looking than some of the female students at Cleek, especially the ones with underarm hair who were studying to be social workers. But he had felt duty bound to purchase one from An Hour In Bed as the company had been generous enough to agree to take him on for a month's work experience, in order to study the manufacture of the subject of his thesis. He would be starting his labours with them tomorrow, but in the meantime there was some labouring to be done with one of their products.

Bouncy Beyoncé was now in repose on Arbuckle's bed, where she had been since he'd removed her from her plain brown paper packaging. He now regarded her again, in the hope that in the meantime her appearance might have improved a little. It hadn't. She still looked quite hideous, quite revolting, and how a man could gain pleasure by having sexual intercourse with such a thing was quite beyond him. He certainly didn't think he'd be going back for seconds.

His intentions had been to have sex with a real woman

first, then compare it with sex with its rubber equivalent. However as it appeared he might not be getting sex with a real woman for a while, if ever, he thought he might just as well tackle the inflatable rubber woman first. He could of course have gone to a prostitute for sex - in fact there was a small grant for that very purpose which could be claimed from the university - but his objections to that way round the problem was that the prostitute would probably make him wear a condom and therefore it would not be a true comparison. (Arbuckle had once heard someone say that having sex whilst wearing a condom was like washing your feet with your socks on and could see why this might be so.)

Bouncy Beyoncé, his new rubber playmate, was about five feet six inches tall. It was the only way in which she remotely resembled a real woman. She had a disproportionately large head in relation to her body and a disproportionately large pair of breasts in relation to her disproportionately large head. The head, onto which a crudely painted one-dimensional face had been stuck - the mouth represented by a crimson red gash of the same hue as the large, round dollop of rouge on each of her cheeks - was framed by a long, platinum blonde, curly wig that looked as though it had seen previous service as settee stuffing. The breasts, pointed and perfectly conical and encased in a gigantic black lace bra, reminded Arbuckle of two traffic cones or a larger version of Madonna's breasts in her 'Material Girl' phase. From there it was all downhill. Thankfully the 'realistic real vagina' promised on the cover of the box was for the moment hidden from view by a tiny red satin thong. However the tiny red thong failed dismally to hide the pubic hair bursting from either side of it like an errant gorse bush. Arbuckle couldn't look at it without wincing as it reminded him of something that had stung him the time he'd been scuba diving in Ibiza.

Bouncy Beyoncé had arrived in a flat pack, a consideration for which Arbuckle had been truly thankful to An Hour In Bed. He was less thankful to them when it came to inflating her. The only things he had ever inflated before were the tyres on his bike and he imagined he would have to do something similar in order to make the inflatable rubber woman suitable for purpose. However there was no pump in the box. Neither were there instructions. He was about to abandon the exercise when he spotted a small valve with a plastic stopper on her back. That must be it, she must inflate like an airbed. He tugged on the stopper. Nothing happened. He tugged again. This time it came out with a satisfyingly loud 'pop'. However the inflatable rubber woman failed to inflate.

He examined the valve. Would his bike pump fit it? He tried it. No, too big. What to do? Maybe he could blow her up by mouth? He tried. Nothing. Two minutes hard blowing had left the inflatable woman as flat as when he'd started and himself gasping for breath. He made a note to mention to the powers-that-be at An Hour In Bed that perhaps their quality control wasn't all it should be, and was about to put Bouncy Beyoncé back in her box, re-parcel her and send her back with a letter of complaint when she suddenly started inflating.

Arbuckle sat back to watch the transformation from flat Bouncy Beyoncé to bouncy Bouncy Beyoncé with a mixture of joy and dread; joy that he would now be able to get on with this vital part of his studies, dread for the same reason.

After about thirty seconds she had reached what Arbuckle considered to be woman-like proportions. However she was still inflating. He wasn't too worried, surmising that she was perhaps meant to be a little larger than average; after all she wouldn't be called Bouncy Beyoncé for nothing. Besides, he liked his women a little on the plump side, he preferred them to have something a man could get hold of.

After another twenty seconds had elapsed there was substantially more than something a man could get hold of as Bouncy Beyoncé was still inflating and by now had reached almost Rubens-like proportions. Ten seconds later she was way past Rubens-like proportions and approaching Goodyear Blimp proportions. Arbuckle, realising something would have to be done about it before she filled the entire room, was looking for something sharp to stick in her in order to arrest her development when she suddenly stopped inflating.

Now, she was hovering over his bed at a height of about six inches, a height which she attained each time he let go of her after laying her down. He had tried placing weights on her to hold her down on the bed - two bags of sugar and a pan of water, no proper weights being to hand - but they had fallen off and all he had achieved was a bag of wet sugar and a sex doll with a sticky stomach. He had thought to tie her down to the bed but hadn't any string or rope. With no other ideas forthcoming he had decided to go ahead with the intercourse as things stood, or perhaps hovered.

He now prepared to make love. He had never made love before but thanks to what he had learned on his coursework and hundreds of porn movies he knew how to go about it, although he thought that on this occasion he'd skip the foreplay. He removed all his clothes, self-consciously glancing at Bouncy Beyoncé just as he might have on undressing in front of a real woman, although not to make the act as realistic as possible, as advised by his tutor, but because he could have sworn she was watching him.

About three-quarters of the way through her over-inflation Bouncy Beyoncé's bra had snapped, departed her breasts, and landed on the television set, where it was now half covering *Loose Women*. In an ideal world Arbuckle would have liked the same thing to have happened to her little red thong, but unfortunately it had remained securely in place. Unlike Tom Hanks' underpants in the film *Big*, as Bouncy Beyoncé's body had got bigger her thong had remained the same size. Consequently it had almost disappeared between her huge thighs and Arbuckle suspected removing it might be a bit tricky. He wasn't wrong.

Ten minutes and twenty attempts later he was no nearer to removing the thong than when he started. He had set about the task by kneeling between Bouncy Beyoncé's legs, then, taking hold of the thin string-like tape at each side of the thong, attempting to pull it down. However as she was floating there was no resistance and when the thong moved down Bouncy Beyoncé moved down with her.

He then adopted the strategy of sitting on her legs, thus mooring her, and going through the same procedure. He had more success with this, inasmuch as the thong started to come down leaving Bouncy Beyoncé where she was, but after he'd pulled it down about six inches he made the mistake of letting it go to have a rest and it had twanged back from whence it came. Resolving to hang on to it the next time he had to stop for a breather, he tried again. But six inches, seven at the most, appeared to be the limit, no matter how much he tugged and how much he rested and hung on to it between tugs. Finally he abandoned the exercise, got a pair of scissors and cut off the thong.

Now unfettered Bouncy Beyoncé's genital area looked to Arbuckle to be less like the sea creature that had once stung him in Ibiza and more like the Black Forest in Bavaria. Providing a background, and complementing the geographic analogy, her breasts looked like a small mountain range. Feeling much as he imagined Bear Grylls felt whenever he ventured into uncharted territory, Arbuckle now prepared to set out on his expedition into the unknown.

Before receiving the inflatable rubber woman Arbuckle had considered by what method he might have sex with one. From his studies and diligent reading of the *Kama Sutra* (one of the set books in his coursework), he had already learned the forty most popular positions in which the act can be performed. He had thought that maybe he'd go for 'girl on top' or possibly 'doggy fashion', having formed the opinion that several of the other positions, although they might prove to be more pleasurable, could only be achieved at the risk of throwing at least one of his limbs out of joint or doing his back in.

He viewed the task ahead with trepidation. He didn't envisage any difficulties in being able to achieve penetration with the 'girl on top' method, but felt that once penetration had been achieved problems might have to be faced in 'hanging on to the girl on top to stop her floating away' method. 'doggy fashion' brought with it the same problem of there being no resistance to his thrusts, as if he were to attempt it he could see nothing ahead of him but the frustration of continually moving up the bed and having to go back and start again.

All things considered he felt that the only sensible method would be the 'missionary position', as if he were to attempt the 'girl on top' or 'doggy fashion' methods both the sex doll, and the problem it now presented in having sex with it, might prove to be insurmountable.

Now straddling Bouncy Beyoncé, he attempted to penetrate her. This was by no means easy as her over-inflated state had rendered her vagina much tighter and thus harder to enter. At first Arbuckle thought the reason he was having difficulty was because he was well-endowed, which induced a little smirk on his face. However it soon disappeared when he recalled that, if anything, he was less well-endowed than most men, if the evidence of what he had seen in men's changing rooms and surreptitious looks in public conveniences whilst urinating were anything to go by.

The reason for the difficulty of course, as Arbuckle quickly worked out, was that the inflatable rubber woman's vastly increased size had had the effect of making her sexual organ much tighter. Vaseline lubricating jelly, borrowed from Jeremy next door, provided the answer, and once coated in the sailor's persuader his penis entered Bouncy Beyoncé more or less easily.

Contrary to his expectations he quite enjoyed having sex with the inflatable rubber woman. In addition to it being very similar to jumping up and down on a bouncy castle, a pastime he had always enjoyed as a child, it had brought him to orgasm, which of course had never happened to him on the bouncy castle, (although he had been told by one of the older boys that if you put your hand in your pocket and held your todger whilst bouncing up and down it was quite possible).

Towards the end, when he was getting quite excited, he fell off Bouncy Beyoncé. a couple of times, which he assumed wouldn't happen when one had intercourse with a real woman. But that proviso apart, he felt that if sex was even better with a real woman than it was with an inflatable rubber woman then the sooner he started having it the better.

Ten minutes later, after another cup of Earl Grey, he returned to his studies.

CHAPTER SIX

"There seems to have been a long gap between the date of my brother's death and his funeral," observed Pugh.

"There was a rather unusual burial request," explained Oldknow. "Certain difficulties had to be overcome in carrying it out."

"An unusual burial request?"

"He wanted to be buried in a vagina."

"In Virginia?" Pugh raised his eyebrows. "What's so unusual about that?" He knew that Aneurin had connections in the southern states of America, and whilst he could see why it might be a bit awkward, not to say inconvenient, burying someone in America who had met his end in Ramsbottom, Lancashire, he could see nothing particularly unusual about it.

The solicitor leaned back in his seat slightly and peered at Pugh over his spectacles. "Not Virginia, Mr Pugh. A vagina."

Pugh wasn't sure he'd heard correctly. "My brother wanted to be buried in a woman's minge?"

Oldknow winced at the crude language of the former Minister for Culture. "I'm afraid so. Not a real one of course. A coffin designed to look like one. He left strict instructions as to its design and construction. He was particularly insistent it should have lots of black pubic hair. 'Like a bush' was his most graphic way of describing it. And real hair. It cost a small fortune."

Pugh didn't at all like the idea of a small fortune being frittered away from his inheritance by the purchase of a coffin that looked like a vagina with real hair. However he was intrigued as to why anyone would want to make such a request in the first place. He asked the solicitor.

Oldknow shrugged. "People get buried in all manner of things nowadays; indeed there are specialist coffin suppliers who cater for the most bizarre of tastes. I once heard of someone being buried in a Red Arrows jet coffin. Another in a motor-bike sidecar, alongside her motor-cyclist husband who had met his demise a year earlier. In your brother Aneurin's case, from what I've been told – although I didn't delve too deeply I must admit - he believed very much in the rejuvenating powers of the vagina."

"Rejuvenating powers?" Pugh was surprised to say the least. "He's not expecting it to bring him back to life, is he?"

Oldknow smiled. "I shouldn't think so. Perhaps revitalising powers would be a more suitable expression. Your brother believed that there was nothing better than sexual intercourse for making a man feel good about himself, giving him a feeling of well-being if you will, a feeling which transposed itself into his everyday life, made him perform his job better, made him a better husband, father and human being."

Pugh nodded. His brother was right, or at least partially right; you did feel a lot better after a good blow through, although whether it made you do your job better afterwards he wasn't so sure. Personally he always wanted to go to sleep immediately after it. He nodded. "Yes, I can see that."

"Apparently he devoted his life to ensuring that as many men as possible gained from his beliefs. And possibly he had such a respect for the role the vagina had played in his life that he wanted to show this respect in death by being buried in one. In fact it was that which caused the delay in his burial. Wacky Caskets, the firm that Oldknow and Wormald charged with supplying the coffin, had trouble getting the right shade of pink velvet for its inner walls. And I believe there was some trouble with the Canadian Redwood clitoris fouling the corpse. In the end they had to settle for positioning it off centre, although I don't suppose your brother minded. All told it was over two weeks before he could be interred."

Pugh visualised his brother lying in his idea of a vagina-shaped coffin. A thought struck him. "How did they carry it?"

"Most gingerly and with great trepidation, I should imagine. I didn't attend the ceremony personally."

It was the contents of the letter marked 'Private and Confidential' that had informed Pugh of his brother Aneurin's death from a heart attack. Pugh didn't like receiving letters marked Private and Confidential; in his experience they rarely contained good news and very often quite the reverse. However he certainly enjoyed receiving the news this one had contained, and with an extra pleasure, as he had truly hated his brother with an intensity that only a younger brother can hate an older brother.

The hatred was rooted in jealousy; when they had been growing up his brother had been cleverer than him, better looking than him, stronger than him, a better athlete than him, better at acquiring money than him, and every time they had an argument, which was frequently, Aneurin would bring the difference of opinion to a conclusion by hitting him over the head with the frying pan. As they had many arguments and Hugh had consequently been hit over the head with the frying pan many times it was a moot point as to whether this had damaged his brain or improved it.

By twelve months the elder of the two brothers, Aneurin was a different kettle of fish altogether than his sibling. Versed by his father in the principals of socialism Aneurin, unlike Hugh, had rejected the dogma out of hand in favour of capitalism. Whereas by the age of eleven Hugh had fully accepted the principle of 'share and share alike' Aneurin at twelve had embraced the less sociable but much more profitable 'what's yours is mine and what's mine's my own'. To his father's great despair whilst Hugh was spending all his spare time distributing Labour Party pamphlets Aneurin was running his own business as a bookies' runner. By the time he left school two years later he was a fully fledged partner in the firm of Potter & Pugh, Turf Accountants. He left home as soon as he was legally able to, at the age of sixteen, and within two years, with the profits from his share of the bookmaking business, had opened one of Nottingham's first night clubs, the *Pink Pussycat*. It was the era when striptease joints and porn magazines began to proliferate. From his offices in the *Pink Pussycat* no one saw that they proliferated more, and with more profit, than Aneurin Pugh. It was only a matter of time before Nottingham wasn't big enough to hold him. At the age of twenty he sold all his interests in the city and departed for the brighter lights and greater opportunities of London. And until receiving the news of his death, apart from a rumour that he had gone to seek even more fortune in America, that was the last Hugh Pugh had heard of his brother. Or wanted to.

The letter from Oldknow and Wormald, Commissioners for Oaths, had informed him of nothing other than that Aneurin had died intestate, along with a request for Pugh to contact the firm's Mr Benjamin Oldknow at his convenience. Pugh's convenience was very quick, no more than two minutes, the time it had taken him to look up the word 'intestate' in the dictionary to confirm that it meant 'without leaving a will', and to pinch himself to confirm he wasn't dreaming. A meeting was arranged for the following day.

Now in the middle of that meeting, and before getting down to the business of Pugh's inheritance, Oldknow filled him in with a few details relevant to his brother's demise.

"At first we had no idea your brother had a brother. It was only when his housekeeper returned from an extended holiday and recalled that he'd mentioned you in passing a couple of times, and we'd followed it up, that we became aware of your existence. Certainly no one at the An Hour In Bed factory in Ramsbottom knew of you."

"He owned a firm who made beds?"

"No. Apparently it's a pun, a play on his name Aneurin - 'An...hour...in...bed'."

Pugh grimaced. "Very droll I'm sure. So what did his firm make?"

"Inflatable rubber women."

"Inflatable rubber women?"

"Apparently your brother maintained the belief that having sex with an inflatable rubber woman was almost as beneficial in creating a feeling of well-being as the real thing. This being the case he viewed his operation more like a public service than a money-making operation. Which isn't to say he didn't make substantial profits from the sales of inflatable rubber women. Which remains the case with An Hour In Bed today, so far as I know."

Pugh's heart beat faster. Substantial profits. What a wonderful coming together of words. "How big are they?"

"Well the usual size I suppose. Although I'm told they do one for dwarfs. Modelled on Disney's *Snow White* I believe."

"Not the fucking inflatable rubber women," Pugh barked impatiently,

"The firm, how big is the firm?"

"Ah. An Hour In Bed is by far the biggest manufacturer of inflatable rubber women in the country. Seventy two per cent of the market, according to their company secretary, Mr Plimmer."

Pugh gave a silent whistle. Seventy two per cent of the market. He wondered what it meant in round figures, or shapely figures with big tits, given the nature of the merchandise. A lot. Must be thousands. Millions. He wouldn't mind betting that most of the men he came into contact with, especially his male compatriots in the House of Commons, had intimate knowledge of inflatable rubber women. As for the Lords....well the sky was the limit. And while it was true that the sexual appetite and tastes of the average man paled into insignificance when compared to those of an MP they didn't pale so far as to disappear completely. And he was now the owner of a business that would be catering for at least part of those tastes! Salvation had arrived. His ship had come in, bringing with it the cargo of an assured future. It didn't matter now if he lost his seat at the next election, check, when he lost his seat at the next election, he would be safeguarded from it, in contempt of it, in clover!

Was there any money to come? In addition to this wonderful thing that had been dropped in his lap? There must be, you don't own by far the biggest inflatable rubber woman factory in the country without earning a bob or two in the process. How much had his brother salted way? A million? More? He could be a multi-millionaire. His heart beat even faster. He could be sitting here in this solicitor's office a multi-millionaire for Christ's sake! He must check out the date of Sotheby's next fine wine auction when he got back to the office, first thing. And fuck fact-finding in The Maldives, it would be fuck-finding anywhere in the world he felt like finding it from now on. In fact he wouldn't have to find it, it would come looking for him waving its knickers.

"Did my brother leave any money?" he now asked, trying not to sound too anxious.

Like all solicitors Oldknow chose to go round the houses before arriving back where he started from and getting to the nitty gritty. "Your brother was a very rich man." Pugh positively beamed. A gloat quickly joined it. "Unfortunately, twelve months ago he gave most of his money away."

Pugh stopped beaming and gloating, a dropped jaw not conducive to exhibiting an expression of unbridled joy. "What do you mean he gave it away?"

"To a university. Cleek University to be precise."

"Cleek University?"

"Perhaps he was an alumni?"

"He was a cunt," snarled Pugh. He slapped his forehead with his hand in anguish. "Christ, giving all his money away to a university for fuck's sake!"

"Well not all his money. There is still a quite substantial inheritance."

Pugh gratefully grabbed hold of the lifeline the solicitor had thrown him. He wasn't going down with the *Titanic* after all; he was Kate Winslett hanging on to the flotsam, not Leonardo de Caprio in the drink freezing his bollocks off. Figures began to go round in his head again, revolving like the numbers on a slot machine, although this time they were modified by his brother's profligacy; two hundred grand, three hundred grand, five hundred grand? Please, please God, let it be five hundred grand. He wasted no further time in finding out. "How much?"

"Sixty thousand pounds, more or less."

Substantial? What was the old fool talking about? He

wants to try living with my outgoings and he'd soon find out how substantial sixty thousand quid is. His mind raced. He must have left something else. Property! A house maybe. The owner of the biggest inflatable rubber woman factory in the country must have had a house, a big house. "How about property?"

"I'm afraid not. Apparently he sold Pugh Manor last year."

Pugh Manor? Christ he'd had a manor. And the twat had sold it! But if he'd sold it, where was the money, what had happened to the proceeds of the sale?

"The money he raised from the sale was part of the ten million pounds he gave to Cleek University," continued Oldknow, strangling Pugh's latest hopes at birth.

Pugh silently cursed his brother for presenting him with a magic carpet to the future then inch by inch pulling it away from under his feet. He shook his head in disbelief. "The bastard. The fucking bastard." He thought for a minute on his words. They were inadequate. "The cocksucking motherfucking twat!" That was better. It didn't make him feel any better though. But Oldknow's next words did.

"An Hour In Bed is still a thriving concern however. If your brother made ten million pounds and a handsome living out of it I've no doubt you will be able to do the same."

*

As his chauffeur Slaithwaite drove him back to London in the Mercedes S 500 Pugh reflected on the solicitor's words. He was right of course. All right, ten million pounds and the largest inflatable rubber woman factory in the country would have been absolutely wonderful, but sixty grand and the largest inflatable rubber woman factory in the country was not to be sniffed at. Especially the department that tested them. The thought of inflatable rubber women being tested for shagworthiness, or whatever the inflatable rubber woman manufacturing equivalent of roadworthiness happened to be, brought forth a guffaw from Pugh.

"Did you say something, sir," asked Slaithwaite.

Pugh thought he'd do a little market research "You're a bachelor aren't you, Slaithwaite?"

"Sir."

"Ever used an inflatable rubber woman?"

"Me sir? No sir. No, I can get all the sex I want with proper women. The uniform helps." Pugh wondered what it was about a chauffeur's uniform that might induce a woman to make free with her favours. He was about to ask when Slaithwaite continued, saving him the bother. "I tell them I'm an officer in the Horseguards. The leather riding boots help. I've been asked to keep them on more than once." He paused. "About inflatable rubber women though. I do have a mate who's into them. If you'll pardon the expression. Swears by them. *Fuck 'em* he says. Sorry sir, just a joke. He does fuck them though, regular. Says they're better than real women; they never have the rag on and they don't moan when you come too quick. I know a couple of other men who use them too. Why do you ask, sir?"

"No reason, Slaithwaite."

"I tell you something though. I wouldn't mind owning the factory that makes them. The man who owns an inflatable rubber woman factory must be a very happy man."

I am, Slaithwaite, I am, thought Pugh, and settled back in the luxurious leather seat of the Mercedes. Even as he did he thought he might change it for the luxurious leather of a Rolls-Royce. The ride home was the happiest he'd had in ages.

CHAPTER SEVEN

Boing...boing...boing...boing...boing...boing...boing.

Cleaver groaned. It was the middle of the third week of his twenty eight days gaol sentence for setting fire to the Body Shop and the end of his incarceration couldn't come soon enough. If a spell locked up in prison is designed to make a man contemplate the act responsible for putting him there, to imbue him with a resolve to keep his nose clean in future, then in Cleaver's case the system was working one hundred per cent efficiently.

Boing...boing...boing...boing...boing...boing...boing.

The sound of the 'boings' was enhanced as it bounced off the hard edges of the gloss painted brick walls. Fine for hi-fi but crap for what I'm being forced to listen to, thought Cleaver, as he rolled his eyes and gritted his teeth in the half light of the cell. He was having just as much trouble with an inflatable rubber woman as Arbuckle had experienced with his, although in this instance the sex doll in question belonged not to him but to his cell mate, Mason.

Boing...boing...boing...moan...boing...boing boing.

"For Christ's sake, Mason, it's three-o-clock in the morning!"

"When a man's got to fuck a man's got to fuck," came Mason's voice from above, quite uncompromisingly and interspersed with further boinging noises from the steel springs of the bunk bed.

It was the first time Cleaver had ever been in prison. He

had heard tales of life behind bars, what could be acquired while you are inside, smuggled in by a visitor or got hold of through a bent screw; booze, cigarettes, drugs, food you could eat, but he had never suspected that inflatable rubber women could be so readily obtained.

Boing...boing...boing....groan...boing...boing...boing..."You're the only one, Baby, you're the only one."

"She's not the only one, there's another one in the fucking bin," said Cleaver, with feeling.

There was too, discarded there by Mason when his new inflatable rubber woman had arrived by post that morning, a necessary replacement after he'd worn out the other one. "They don't make 'em like they used to," he had complained. "I've only had it six months, the one I had in the Scrubs lasted me two years."

Two days after he'd been sent down Cleaver had asked for a transfer to another cell. From the cell in which his cellmate had a chronic farting problem. This was the cell he'd landed up in. The following day he would have given his right arm to be returned to the cell he'd briefly shared with Farting Fred. He would have happily shared a cell with ten Farting Freds but prison policy dictated that a prisoner could only request one change of cell and he had already exhausted his quota.

Boing...moan...boing...groan...boing...moan...boing.

"Good, the moans and groans are getting more frequent," Cleaver said to himself, now familiar with the pattern of Mason's lovemaking. "He's getting close to the vinegar stroke, won't be long now thank Christ. Then maybe I can get some shuteye."

The noise from above suddenly stopped. But surprisingly without the extended moan, followed by a huge sigh of contentment, with which Mason usually reached his climax.

Cleaver wondered why. Had Mason by some unfortunate chance died? Make that fortunate. Could it be that he'd had a heart attack whilst doing the business with Moist Moira? Cleaver had never wished death on anyone but he wished it on Mason right now. He sat up, put his hand to his ear in the time-honoured manner and listened for a few seconds. Shit. He could hear breathing. So the bastard hadn't died after all. But at least the sex was over, the boings and the moans and the groans had ended and his tormentor was almost silent now; wonderfully, peacefully silent. Cleaver breathed a sigh of relief, lay down again, pulled the blanket up over him, snuggled up in the foetal position, muttered "Thank Christ that's over with for another night," and prepared to be welcomed into the arms of Morpheus.

"I haven't finished yet."

"What the....?" Cleaver sat bolt upright. Morpheus would have to wait for him a bit longer. "What did you just say?"

"I haven't finished yet."

"What? Why have you stopped then?"

"I'm making it last."

Cleaver was gob-smacked. "What for?"

"You know, like you do with a real woman. To satisfy her. I read it in 'Loaded'. The bloke said if you make it last longer she'll enjoy it more and if she enjoys it more you'll enjoy it more."

Cleaver could scarcely believe his ears. "It's a lump of rubber for Christ's sake!"

"Not to me it isn't."

Boing...boing...boing...moan...boing...boing...boing.

Cleaver slapped his forehead with the heel of his hand in despair. The moans were back to their normal level. And no groans. It went moans on their own, then moans and groans, but Mason was back to moans on their own again. How much longer was he going to be at it?

"What can I think about?" called Mason, over Cleaver's thoughts and the sound of the last two boings.

"What?"

"It said if you think about something else you can make it last longer."

"Think about what a twat you are."

The box containing Moist Moira, one of An Hour In Bed's super-de-luxe models - *'She'll never let you down and we'll bet you never let her down'* - also contained a brochure which listed the full range of the firm's sex dolls. With nothing to read, having finished his library book, *Escape from Cell Thirteen*, and having read for the twentieth time the Prison Rules posted on the cell wall above the lavatory (so you had something to read while you were pissing, Cleaver had surmised), and also having read the graffiti on the cell walls for the twentieth time, the pick of which was *'Prison Rules!'*, Cleaver had glanced through An Hour In Bed's literature. Bloody disgusting. He had a repugnance of all sex toys but a hatred of inflatable rubber women in particular. Bloody hell, they had one now with a realistic anus. It wasn't enough to have a realistic fanny, after you'd fucked her you could turn her over and give her one up the arse!

Inflatable rubber women hadn't had such refinements back in the days when as a ten-year-old he'd stumbled across his father astride one; when he had innocently informed his mother of his father's hobby by asking her what daddy was doing; when she had then seen for herself what daddy was doing and promptly walked out on him and left Cleaver motherless, with only his pervert of a father to bring him up.

Boing...boing...boing...moan...boing...boing...boing...."I'm thinking about Man U. Wayne Rooney's just taking a penalty to win the European Cup in the last minute of injury time."

"Well I hope he fucking misses."

Boing...boing...boing...moan...boing...boing...boing.

Christ I don't think I'll be able to take another ten days of this, thought Cleaver. But he would have to take it. He'd lived up to Mrs Wisbech's forecast and early release was now out of the question. He'd kicked that in the head when he'd called the Governor a twat for refusing to do anything about Mason. "It keeps him quiet," the Governor had said, when Cleaver complained about the nocturnal missions and emissions of his cellmate.

"Quiet?" echoed Cleaver. "He's making more noise up there than a road drill. He sounds like a road drill. When he's not sounding like a sludge pump."

"As long as it's occupying his mind I couldn't care less what he sounds like," the Governor had replied, unimpressed by Cleaver's observation. He was fully aware of how much trouble the minds of serial offenders like Mason could dream up if their thoughts weren't engaged elsewhere. "He has a history of violence."

"I'll have a history of violence if you don't do something about it," Cleaver had warned. But it hadn't cut any ice; Mason had three years remaining of his sentence, Cleaver had little over a week, the Governor knew which one of them he wanted to keep happy. And there wasn't much chance of Cleaver starting a history of violence, as he had threatened he might, at least not violence on Mason; his cellmate was a much bigger, harder man, otherwise Cleaver would have duffed him up already.

"He's scored! Rooney's scored! We've won the cup, we've won the cup, ee–i-addio we've won the cup."

Boing...boing...boing...moan...boing...boing...boing.

Mason and his rubber lover finally finished their exertions just before four-o-clock, Mason apparently having run out of things to think about. Now unable to sleep, a situation not made any more tolerable by Mason snoring his fool head off, Cleaver began to think about what he would do when this nightmare was over and he was released. Lots. His first priority would be to shake up those Mary Anns at VAST. Shake them out of their lethargy and get them going, get them moving. Bollocks to sending letters to people asking them to stop buying sex toys, it was time for a more positive approach. And he was the one to supply it.

CHAPTER EIGHT

The tour by Hugh Pugh of his newly inherited inflatable rubber woman factory had been going quite well until he was asked by Wainwright if he would like to take a break for a coffee before or after they visited the Realistic Vaginal Juices Department.

Pugh had dined in the works canteen on a rather greasy mutton cobbler only an hour earlier and the thought of what the Realistic Vaginal Juices Department might contain, coupled with the rustic fare he had eaten, caused his already dodgy stomach to turn over and a small amount of vomit to find its way into his mouth. His attempt to swallow it might have been more successful had there not been a bit more cobbler coming up. The resultant collision between the two, with the concomitant cutting off of his air supply, had caused him to cough and splutter.

"Are you all right, Mr Pugh," said Wainwright, concerned. Up until now the new owner's visit had been wholly satisfactory. The factory manager was anxious to keep it that way. Pugh was largely an unknown quantity and Wainwright feared the worse. The only time Aneurin Pugh had ever mentioned his brother, at the time the Transport Minister was attempting to push through a deeply flawed piece of road traffic legislation, he had referred to him as 'that pillock of a brother of mine'.

As yet however, Pugh hadn't shown any signs of living up to Aneurin's opinion of him. Indeed he had been quite affable. The only untoward incident had been when one of the girls in the Dyeing and Tinting Department had approached with a piece of paper in her hand and had shyly said to him: "Can I have your autograph please?" Pugh had stopped and smiled at her. "I've always been a big fan of yours, Mr Lloyd Webber," the girl continued. Pugh had glared at her and told her to bugger off and get on with her work and bloody quick before he gave her the sack.

Pugh quickly collected himself and brushed off the stomach-churning vomit-inducing incident as though it had never happened. "Wind. Pastry, it always does for me," he informed Wainwright, forcefully; the last thing he wanted to do was exhibit any signs of weakness in front of his newly-acquired minions. He intended to rule his new factory with a rod of iron, to start as he meant to go on.

"Oh dear," said Wainwright. "Perhaps you should have gone for the tripe, cowheel and onion fricassee, it's a big favourite in Ramsbottom."

His mind still half on the Realistic Vaginal Juices Department Pugh's stomach turned another somersault at the mention of the canteen's alternative lunch offering, big favourite in Ramsbottom or no. Apart from that he'd already had his fill of ram's bottoms with the mutton. At this point he decided to bail out in case the factory manager had anything worse up his sleeve, sheep's entrails on a bed of silage possibly. "I think I'll call it a day, Wainwright," he said. "I've already seen far more than I can fully take in during a single visit."

And he had. He'd seen the Mixing Department, where the constituent elements of the rubber solution from which the inflatable rubber women were manufactured were blended together; the Dyeing and Tinting Department, which dyed the rubber pink or various shades of brown; the Forming Department, which extruded the rubber solution into a basic rubber woman shape; the Breasts Department (where he had been shown the new novelty breasts, a pair of tits with 'Ant' written on one and 'Dec' on the other); the Improving Room, which trimmed and bonded the pairs of large breasts to the rubber women; (when Pugh had commented that all the rubber women seemed to have large breasts Wainwright had explained that they had once introduced a small-breasted rubber woman but of the one thousand manufactured and offered for sale nine hundred and ninety eight had remained unsold); the Head and Face Department, which moulded the heads for the rubber women, stuck a variety of faces on them and fitted them with a wig; the Painting Department, which painted lips and eyes and rouge on the faces and black leather boots on the legs of the budget models that weren't to be equipped with real black leather boots; the Sexual Organ Department (known both as SOD, and, colloquially, the Pussy Room, judging by the chalk handwriting on the door), where the inflatable rubber women's vaginas were made; the Genital Fitting Department, where they were fitted; and a few other departments which Pugh had already forgotten about.

The main factory itself had been built around the beginning of the twentieth century as a small single story calico printing works. Since An Hour In Bed had taken over the premises in 1972 many extensions to the original building had been made to cope with the ever increasing demand for the company's product, and although the many departments were still housed under one roof the interior of the factory resembled a labyrinth.

Pugh had been surprised at the size and scope of the operation. Including the management the factory had a workforce of 110. An average of five thousand two hundred inflatable rubber women were made every week and sold in seventy three different countries. The prices ranged from £12.50 to £180, with an average of £45. Pugh quickly worked out, 5200 multiplied by 45, that this meant the factory was pulling in £212,000 a week, mathematics being his strong subject (although not quite strong enough as the correct total was £234,000). Additional revenue was generated by guided tours of the factory (free, but healthy post-tour sales and catering); a Factory Shop where 'pick your own' customers could take advantage of a twenty per cent discount; a monthly Farmer's and Inflatable Rubber Woman's Market (apparently inflatable rubber women were big with the local farming community, so the two were natural bed mates); and the Visitor Centre, which featured a half-hour video of the manufacturing process along with the opportunity to custom-make your own inflatable rubber woman.

Pugh had thought that men would be attracted to working at an inflatable rubber woman factory like flies to a jam pot, so it came as a surprise to him when Wainwright informed him that the majority of the workforce was female. After mulling it over he hazarded a guess, which he voiced to Wainwright, that the reason might be because if they employed men they would probably spend half their time shagging the inflatable rubber women instead of making more of them. Wainwright knew to the contrary however, and informed Pugh that although a few men had taken advantage of both their position and the inflatable rubber women, especially the top-of-the-range models with realistic vaginal juices, it never lasted for very long.

It was the 'sweet factory syndrome', he explained, whereby workers new to a sweet factory could hardly keep their hands off the sweets for the first day or so but thereafter largely left them alone. The same applied to male inflatable rubber women workers.

He went on to tell Pugh that the reason over eighty per cent of the workforce was female was simply because most of the jobs were part time, which suited women more than men, and suited the management because they could pay them much lower wages. Pugh beamed on being given this news; he was one hundred per cent in favour of lower wages, especially when it was his pocket they would be coming out of.

Pugh also learned that not only was An Hour In Bed the largest supplier of inflatable rubber women in the country but also the second largest in the world. (Molls Unlimited in America was the largest); that in 2008 the firm had won the *Queen's Award for Enterprise* (but had been asked to keep quiet about it); and that inflatable rubber women were the company's sole product.

When car air bags had first been introduced Aneurin Pugh had toyed with the idea of getting into what was obviously going to be a large and lucrative market but had eventually decided against it, possibly feeling that an inflatable rubber woman suddenly emerging from the dashboard on impact would probably be a greater shock to the driver's system than the crashing of their car.

Dirigibles and weather balloons had also been considered. A prototype weather balloon had actually been made, in the shape of a one hundred and twenty feet long inflatable rubber woman (enabling it to double as a giant advert for the company's product), but the project had been abandoned after pranksters had cut its guy ropes and it had disappeared into the night. It was reported a month later that after apparently getting a slow puncture after passing through a hail storm it had eventually come to earth in one of the more remote Solomon Islands, where the natives were now worshipping it as a fertility goddess.

Passing through the warehouse on the way to the Secondhand, Organ Renewal and Refurbishment Department, Pugh had been surprised at the very high stock levels, palette upon palette of flat-pack boxes stacked to a height of fifty feet or more. However he hadn't commented on this to Wainwright, crediting him with knowing what he was doing.

"What time did you say the company secretary would be back?" Pugh now asked the factory manager.

"Mr Plimmer? He said he'd try to get back for around four-thirty."

"He is aware of my visit?"

"Oh yes."

"Where did you say he'd gone?"

"I don't think I did."

Pugh waited for Wainwright to tell him. He showed no signs of doing so. Pugh fixed him with a baleful stare. Were they all this bloody thick at An Hour In Bed? If they were he'd soon be having a big sort out, the big stick would have to come out, by Christ would it. "So where has this Plimmer character gone to then, or is it a secret?"

"No. No of course not. He had to go to the Inland Revenue office and the VAT people."

"Really?" Pugh was immediately suspicious; company secretaries aren't summoned to Inland Revenue and VAT offices for nothing. He narrowed his eyes. "I hope there's nothing wrong?"

"I'm afraid you'll have to ask Mr Plimmer that," said Wainwright, guardedly.

"I intend to."

Pugh only just got the chance to question Plimmer as the

company secretary didn't get back until it had turned five-fifteen. The factory and offices closed for the day at five-thirty and Pugh was about to give up the ghost and head back for London when Plimmer finally arrived. Ten minutes later he was wishing he had never arrived.

CHAPTER NINE

After his initial tryst with the inflatable rubber woman Elton Arbuckle had sex a further six times that week, only four of them with Bouncy Beyoncé.

After giving it a great deal of thought, and although he didn't like the idea, he came to the decision that the only way he was going to able to compare sex with an inflatable rubber woman and sex with a real woman was to avail himself of the services of a prostitute. He accepted that the prostitute would probably make him wear a condom, but figured that as both the inflatable rubber woman and the condom were made of rubber the comparison would provide a more accurate comparison than having sex with a woman who didn't make him wear a condom. Subsequently he drew the £50 grant available for this purpose from the university bursar. An avuncular type, the bursar also advised him on the best place to pick up a prostitute (a service he happily supplied to the university's students, whether they were from the Department of Sex and Inflatable Rubber Woman Studies or any of the other forty departments).

"Let's get the unpleasant business over with first shall we?" the prostitute said to Arbuckle, as soon as they'd entered the bedroom.

"Oh I don't think it will be unpleasant," said Arbuckle with a smile. "Not for me at least. Although I appreciate it might get to be a bit unpleasant for you sometimes, having to do it all day," he added, considerately.

The prostitute looked him up and down, unsure whether he was joking or not. She must have decided he wasn't as she held out her hand for the money. Arbuckle, not expecting this, but never having had sex with a prostitute and uncertain of its protocols and traditions, shook it.

The prostitute eyed him for a moment. He was definitely from another planet, the only question was which one. She freed her hand and held it out again. "The money," she said, in a no-nonsense voice, in case Arbuckle was thinking of shaking it again.

"Ah. Of course. You see I was thinking you paid after," he explained.

"I'm a prostitute not a restaurant."

"Yes," said Arbuckle, colouring up a little. He took the fifty pounds out of his wallet. "How much is it?"

"Is it just straight sex or do you want any extras?"

"Extras?" The only extras Arbuckle had ever heard of were those that were added to cricket scores and he couldn't imagine she was talking about leg byes or wides.

"Like I could sit on your face."

Arbuckle thought it highly unlikely that such a service was offered at Lord's. Even if it was he couldn't see why anyone would require it. "Why would I want you to do that?" he asked.

She shrugged. "A lot of men do."

Arbuckle tried hard but couldn't come up with a single reason why a man would want a woman to sit on his face, and several reasons why he wouldn't, the main one being that she might fart. "I think I'll pass on that," he said. "If you don't mind," he added politely.

"I don't mind at all love, whatever turns you on. It's thirty pounds or forty pounds bareback." She saw Arbuckle's puzzled look. "And I don't mean doing it while we're riding a horse, I mean without a condom."

"Ah." Arbuckle brightened at this bonus. "Yes, without a condom please."

She looked him up and own, a little unsure. "You are clean are you?"

The Sex part of the Sex and Inflatable Rubber Woman Studies degree course had informed Arbuckle that 'clean' in this context meant free from sexually transmitted diseases. So he didn't embarrass himself by saying that yes, he was clean, he'd had a shower that morning. However he did embarrass himself when he'd handed over the forty pounds and she'd started removing her clothes and asked him how he wanted her.

"Well I was thinking of on the bed. If that's possible?"

She shook her head slowly. "Are you real or what?"

"Or on the floor if you prefer. I'm really not fussed either way."

"I meant which way? Which way do you want me?"

Arbuckle thought about it for a moment. In truth he didn't really have a preference. "Well with your head at the headboard end I suppose," he said finally. Then, thinking he might be missing something, "Unless it's better the other way up. I mean I wouldn't want to miss out on anything."

The prostitute regarded him again, still not at all sure whether he was joking. She didn't like jokers; the verbal jokes she could stand but jokers could get up to some funny things once the sex had started, a girl had to be careful; she'd once had a circus clown who halfway through had stuck a toy trumpet up her bottom and started squeezing her breasts in a vain attempt to make a noise like the horn on his collapsing car. She decided to take a chance on him. "I meant on my back or on my belly."

"Oh. Sorry. You see it's the first time I've ever.....you

know...."

"I'd never have guessed."

"Thank you." He came to a decision. "Well then, on your back, please."

They had sex. Arbuckle judged that it was very similar, and certainly no better, than having sex with an inflatable rubber woman, although if he'd had to award points out of ten he would have given six to the prostitute and eight to the inflatable rubber woman on the grounds that the inflatable rubber woman had been slightly less passive and hadn't kept yawning.

Jolene, the student Arbuckle had sex with the following night, didn't yawn while they were having it, but only because she never stopped talking.

When he first arrived at Cleek Arbuckle quickly learned that the best place to pick up girls was in the bar of the Students Union. He had tried his luck there from time to time, but while he had witnessed the slinking off to have sex of many newly paired students he had never managed to slink off to have sex with one himself, and had long since given up hopes of ever doing so. These days he just used the bar for the occasional relaxing pint of beer after his daily studies. So it was completely unexpected when after getting his pint of Theakston's Old Peculier from the bar, and settling with it at a corner table, that Jolene walked up to him and asked him if he'd like a fuck. Arbuckle said he'd like a fuck very much indeed and five minutes later they were having one in her room. Arbuckle would have liked to know why, from amongst the other twenty or so male students in the bar at the time, she had selected him, so that if it was because of the irresistible manner in which he had been lounging nonchalantly at the table he could work on developing it in the hope of tempting other girls into coming up to him and asking him if he'd like a fuck. However he hadn't asked her in case she changed her mind. Nor, for the same reason, did he ask her why she activated the kitchen timer on the bedside cabinet before inviting him to join her on the bed.

Soon afterwards, when he entered her, she immediately said: "Ask me how it is for me."

"How is it for you?" Arbuckle dutifully replied.

"How do you think it is for me?"

"I've no idea. I've never really thought about it."

"I see. Why do you think you've never thought about it?"

"Is it a bit like poking your finger up your bottom?"

"Have you ever poked your finger up your bottom?"

"Once or twice. When I was younger."

"Why do you think you did that?"

"I don't know. To see what it felt like."

"Do you think it might be because you wondered what it might be like for a homosexual to have a penis up his bottom?"

"It might have been."

"Could it be that you wanted to know what it felt like for a girl to have a penis up her vagina?"

"It might have been that too."

"Did you tell your mother you'd been putting your finger up your bottom?"

"Why would I do that?"

"Maybe you wanted her to know you'd been putting your finger up your bottom because you wanted to know what it felt like for a girl to have a penis up her vagina. In the hope she might offer to let you put your penis up her vagina to find out."

Arbuckle looked at her sharply. "Are you suggesting I

wanted to have sex with my mother?"

"Do you want to have sex with your mother?"

"Of course I don't want...."

A bell rang out. "Time's up," interrupted Jolene. She disengaged herself from Arbuckle and switched off the timer. She turned to him and smiled. "Same time next week?"

It wasn't until a few days later, when Arbuckle had asked around and discovered that Jolene was a psychiatry student, that he realised she'd been practising her psychoanalysing technique on him, and had done the same thing with at least half the male students on the campus. He had smiled ruefully and thought that if he'd known at the time he would have gone along with the deception and given her the ten pounds he had left over from his visit to the prostitute as her consultation fee.

Both the sex with the prostitute and the sex with Jolene were far less satisfying than the four sessions of sex he subsequently had with Bouncy Beyoncé. For one thing you didn't have to pay Beyoncé. every time you wanted to have sex with her; for another she didn't practise psychiatry on you and accuse you of wanting to have sex with your mother, two enormous bonus points in Arbuckle's books. Plus the fact that sex with Bouncy Beyoncé had got progressively more satisfying as the week unfolded.

By pricking her with a pin and allowing an amount of air to escape he had reduced her to what he imagined to be more like her correct proportions. It now felt like he was astride a real woman. If he closed his eyes it was just like being with a real woman. Even if he kept his eyes open it was no worse than looking at Jolene or the prostitute (Bouncy Beyoncé certainly looked more interested than either of them), although if he could have had his time over again he would have chosen somewhere other than her nose to prick the hole as the Blu-Tack he'd had to put over it to stop her deflating any further looked like a particularly big bogie, and put him off a bit.

Like Slaithwaite's mate he found several other advantages an inflatable rubber woman had over a real woman; they never had a headache, as he had heard that women, especially wives, are prone to get around bedtime; you didn't have buy her flowers, or remember her birthday, or take her to the pictures when you'd rather stay in and read a book or something; nor all the other things he'd heard of that men have to put up with in order to have their way with their wives and girlfriends once in a while.

All things considered Arbuckle felt that having an inflatable rubber woman as a bed partner was a far better proposition than relying on her human sister. In fact he couldn't see why he would need to bother a real woman ever again.

CHAPTER TEN

"Are you married, Mr Seal?"

"Oh yes. Yes indeed."

"Happily married?"

Seal looked sharply at the insurance investigator seated opposite him in the dustsheet-covered remains of one of the Seals' easy chairs. "I don't really see what that's got to do with it, if you don't mind me saying so."

"Relax, Mr Seal," said Reamer. "I'm an ex-copper myself. Detective Sergeant. Thirty years."

Seal might have guessed. Many ex-policemen on being pensioned off from the police force took on insurance investigation jobs. However if Reamer's admission was designed to put Seal at his ease it had quite the opposite effect; being an ex-policeman himself he knew what devious bastards they could be.

In fact Seal was far from happily married. The best he could have claimed for his marriage was that it was tolerable. But he wasn't going to admit that to an insurance investigator, even if it was any of his business, which it wasn't. Even so he had to be careful. It was probably on this man's say-so whether or not his claim would be met in full, although personally he would be hard pressed to come up with a reason why it shouldn't be.

"Very happily married," he said, in reply to Reamer's probing. "Why do you ask?"

"We will get to that in the fullness of time." As he said this the man from the Rest Assured Insurance Society smiled portentously. Seal didn't like the smile at all, it reminded him of the smile the appalling SS Jew hunter adopted in *Inglourious Basterds* when he was questioning a suspect.

The insurance claim that had prompted Reamer's visit had been lodged by Seal two weeks previously. Seal had been living at his current address, a semi-detached in Littleover, for just a couple of months, having had to vacate his police house on retirement from the force. When the Seals had moved in there had been an electric fire in the living room hearth. Although appreciating the instant heat and convenience of an electric fire Mrs Seal had asked her husband to disconnect it as she preferred the cosy warmth of a coal fire. Seal had quite happily gone along with her request, the benefits of a nice coal fire being one of the few things on which he and his wife were in accord. In particular he liked to gaze into it on a long winter evening and pick out the faces it accidentally sculpted from its embers. In his previous home he had once picked out two of the Beatles on the same night, although it's true to say that his wife had only recognised John Lennon, she herself being of the opinion that the ember he claimed resembled Ringo Starr looked more like, appropriately enough, Thomas the Tank Engine.

A fire had been laid and lighted and in next to no time had been roaring up the chimney. He and Mrs Seal had pulled up armchairs at each side of the fire to bathe in its warm cosiness, and possibly see another Beatle, or maybe the Fat Controller. Ten minutes later the room was no less warm, but certainly a lot less cosy, when an enormous explosion caused the chimney breast to cave in, instantly transforming the living room into something reminiscent of downtown Beirut.

"You are a member of Vigilantes Against Sex Toys, I believe?" Reamer's question was delivered more as an accusation than an inquiry. It prompted Seal to look guiltily at the door. Reamer was onto it in an instant. "What's the matter?"

"Nothing. Nothing at all," said Seal, trying not to look flustered.

"That isn't the reaction of someone with nothing to hide, Mr Seal. It is the reaction of someone who doesn't want the only other person likely to be in his abode, namely his 'happily married' wife, to know his business."

Seal shook his head vigorously. Both as a denial of Reamer's accusation and because he was at a loss to make any sense of the way the interview was going, which wasn't at all the way he'd imagined it would.

The estimate for the cost of repairs to the damage to the chimney breast and the burned furnishings from the resultant fire was in excess of thirty thousand pounds. This being the case he hadn't expected the insurance man to merely come along and rubber stamp the claim. But by the same token neither had he expected the third degree and insinuations about the state of his marriage. "Why should I have something to hide?" he said, now making this point.

"Everyone's got something to hide, Mr Seal," said Reamer. He tapped the side of his nose with an index finger. "What I'm interested in is why you hid it. Your motivation." He spread his upturned hands. "Well actually I know why you hid it. What I want to know is why you even had it to hide in the first place, if, as you claim, you are a happily married man?"

Seal was now completely at a loss. "Hide what? What am I supposed to have hidden?"

"You tell me."

Seal shook his head in wonderment. "I really don't know what you're talking about, Mr Reamer. Really."

Reamer smiled his Jew hunter smile again. "No, of course you don't." He sat back and produced a silver cigarette case. "Do you mind if I smoke?"

Seal did but he wasn't going to stop him. "No. Feel free."

Reamer opened the cigarette case. He looked at it ruefully for a second or so, shrugged, and indicated it to Seal. "My retirement present. I think they're hoping I'll smoke myself to death so they don't have to pay my pension." He smiled. "Just joking." He offered the cigarette case to Seal. "Would you like one?"

"I don't."

"I know."

Seal almost asked Reamer that if he knew he didn't smoke then why had he asked. But then thought better of it, suspecting it was just another of the investigator's mind games, a ploy to help break him down; although why he should want to break him down he hadn't the faintest idea.

Taking all the time in the world about it Reamer selected a cigarette, tapped it a few times on the case, lighted it with the cigarette case's matching lighter, drew deeply on it, exhaled the smoke high in the air, sat back even further in the chair, made himself comfortable, and regarded Seal, smiling that smile of his all the while. Seal had never felt so uncomfortable in his life. Finally Reamer spoke.

"Why are you a member of VAST?"

"VAST? What's wrong with that?"

"Well if you're anything like the miscreant who recently set fire to the Body Shop, quite a bit."

"I'm not. That was nothing to do with me."

"So you would have us believe."

"It's the truth."

"Maybe." Reamer drew deeply on the cigarette again

before continuing. "But you are, I take it, against the use of sex toys?"

"Yes. Yes of course I am," said Seal, but without any great conviction.

In fact Seal had no strong feelings about sex toys one way or the other, although if pushed he would have come out against them rather than for. He had never used a sex toy in his life, or even contemplated using one. Even if he had he doubted very much that his wife would be a willing partner if using one required her co-operation. He did however have very strong feelings about belonging, being part of. To this end he belonged to the local male voice choir, the amateur dramatic society, the bridge club, the darts team at *The Grim Jogger*, and he was a member of 'The Flatfoot Four', the team composed of policemen and ex-policemen who took part in the weekly pub quiz held there. One night after a quiet post-quiz chat and a pint with the quizmaster Father Flannery, the cleric had mentioned that he was a member of VAST. Seal had expressed interest and it had taken little persuasion from Flannery to get him to join the organisation. It got him out of the house, didn't cost him anything, and gave him yet another thing to belong to.

Reamer hadn't missed the lack of conviction in Seal's reply. "You don't sound very sure about your opposition to sex toys?"

Seal tried to sound more convincing. "I'm very sure."

The insurance investigator looked at him for a moment or two as though making up his mind whether or not to believe him, then said: "I will give you the benefit of the doubt."

Seal decided it was about time he stood up for himself a bit. He hadn't done anything wrong, despite this man's insinuations, and if Reamer thought he had well let him go ahead and prove it. "There isn't any doubt, Mr Reamer. No doubt at all."

"Which I am quite prepared to believe," said Reamer. He smiled. "If you can answer to my satisfaction one question. And that question is this. If, as you say, you are a happily married man, why were you hiding an inflatable rubber woman up your chimney?"

Seal couldn't have been more surprised if Reamer had accused him of having the Crown Jewels hidden up his chimney. "An inflatable rubber woman?"

Reamer opened his briefcase, took out four small pieces of charred rubber, the largest of them no more than four inches by three inches. He took his time in placing them on the coffee table that separated him from Seal, laying them out like exhibits in the Black Museum, then sat back, indicated the pieces of rubber with a nod of his head and invited him to comment.

Seal looked at them more closely. "What are they?"

"You tell me."

"I can't. That's why I'm asking you."

"Very well, if you insist on making things more difficult for yourself than they already are. It is an inflatable rubber woman."

"That? That's an inflatable rubber woman?"

"The remains of. Which were found amongst the resultant debris following the demolition of your chimney breast. Which, I am reliably informed, exploded by virtue of gases building up in your chimney due to it being blocked up by the said inflatable rubber woman."

Seal looked more closely at the pieces of rubber. "They could be anything. They could be from an old inner tube or something."

"They could be, but they're not." He pointed to one of the pieces of rubber. Unlike the other three pieces it had retained some of its pink colouring and in its centre was a round, more pinker protrusion. "Or if they are then it's the first inner tube I've ever seen with a nipple." He indicated another of the pieces of rubber. "And if that isn't conclusive enough evidence, there is this." He pointed out four just discernible words embossed on the rubber. "An Hour In Bed. The name of the manufacturer of the said inflatable rubber woman. The manufacturer from who you purchased it."

"I never did!"

"Then what was it doing up your chimney?"

"Well I didn't put it there," Seal protested.

"So who did?"

"Well I don't know, do I." No sooner had he said this than the answer suddenly came to him. He blurted it out, relieved. "The previous owner. It must have been put there by the previous owner. It would be him, what was his name, Barker, Mr Barker." Another thought came to him, adding strength to his contention. "He was a bachelor."

Reamer raised his eyebrows. "Was he now?" His tone was steeped in suspicion.

Seal picked up on this and furiously nodded agreement. "Yes, a bachelor. A man who would have the need of an inflatable rubber woman. Unlike a married man, a happily married man, like me. Who would not have the need of an inflatable rubber woman."

Reamer nodded. "He lived on his own, this bachelor?"

"Yes. On his own. There were no parents or lodgers or anything."

Reamer smiled, not his Jew hunter faux friendly smile now but a genuine smile of relief that the claimant, a fellow ex-policeman, was off the hook. "Well that would seem to wrap it up then, Mr Seal."

Seal breathed a sigh of relief. "Yes."

"And means of course that I will be able to recommend that your claim is met in full."

"Excellent. Thank you. Thank you indeed, Mr Reamer."

"If you can answer me one more question."

"Of course."

Ominously the genuine smile disappeared from Reamer's face to be replaced by the Jew hunter smile yet again. He toyed with Seal for a few moments. Finally he spoke. "If this character Mr Barker was a bachelor - who, by your own admission, lived on his own - why did he have to hide his inflatable rubber woman up the chimney?"

Seal couldn't supply an answer to Reamer's question, either then or later when he'd had time to think about it. The file was still open but he realised there was little chance his claim would be met. There had been no help forthcoming from Barker when Seal had tracked him down. The former owner of Seal's house had denied all knowledge of the inflatable rubber woman, no doubt thinking that to admit it would lay the blame for the explosion at his door, and when Seal had persisted he had sent him away with a flea in his ear.

CHAPTER ELEVEN

"Are you trying to tell me it's worth fuck all?"

"Well I wouldn't put it quite like that," said the An Hour In Bed company secretary, George Plimmer.

Pugh was steaming. "Then which way would you put it?" Before Plimmer had the chance to tell him Pugh had thought of something. "Surely the land and buildings must be worth something?"

"Oh indeed. But unfortunately Mr Pugh....your brother, that is...remortgaged all the land and buildings in order to partially finance his grand scheme. You do know about the ten million pounds he gave to Cleek University?"

"Don't remind me."

"If only it wasn't for the contaminated stock. If it hadn't been for that...." Plimmer shrugged.

Pugh's head jerked. "What contaminated stock?"

"You didn't pass through the warehouse on your tour of the factory with Mr Wainwright?"

"I did. And it looked pretty overfull to me."

"And he didn't tell you about the contaminated stock?"

Pugh shook his head. "You tell me."

Plimmer looked extremely uncomfortable. "Well strictly speaking Mr Wainwright is the man who should be telling you, it isn't my...."

Pugh gave Plimmer the benefit of the icy glare he reserved for dogsbodies. "Tell me about the contaminated stock!"

Plimmer swallowed. "Yes. Of course. Well the thing is, one million of our inflatable rubber women, which were bound for Africa, have...."

"Africa?"

"Yes. It was by far the biggest order we've ever taken on. Mr Pugh...Aneurin Pugh...it was his idea actually - a very clever man, your brother, if I may say so, brilliant head for business...."

"For Christ's sake get on with it man!"

"Yes. Well Mr Pugh negotiated the order with the African League of Nations along with the Government and a consortium of various charities. I believe War on Want and Oxfam were involved. Your brother's vision was that instead of supplying condoms to African natives, which apparently they don't like to use any more than do men in this country, we would supply them with a million inflatable rubber women; the idea being that they could have intercourse with them instead of having it with their wives and consequently getting them pregnant again, as I believe Africans are prone to do."

"And?"

"And thus adding to the already impoverished population yet another mouth to feed."

"I know that Plimmer, I'm a Cabinet Minister, I'm not fucking thick. I meant and what happened? Why are they still in the warehouse instead of Bongobongoland or wherever we're sending them to?"

"Well as I've already said, they're all contaminated."

"In what way?"

"Apparently some foreign matter or other got in the mixer in the Realistic Vaginal Juices Department and contaminated the realistic vaginas. Then when the realistic vaginas were fitted to the inflatable rubber women they further contaminated the rubber and...well I'm afraid they've all ended up completely unusable. The slightest skin contact with them brings one out in the most terrible rash. Our head of Quality Control, Mr Diplock, is still off work three weeks after becoming contaminated. The poor man simply can't stop scratching. Payment for the rubber women was strictly on delivery, we can't deliver, so...." Plimmer shrugged again.

"Shit!"

"Indeed."

Pugh saw a straw and clutched it. "Can't they keep their clothes on and wear a condom?"

"Well that would rather be defeating the object of sending them inflatable rubber women in the first place, wouldn't it. Besides, as I've already pointed out, they don't like wearing condoms. And as far as keeping their clothes on they don't tend to wear much more than a loincloth in Namibia."

"Shit!"

"Indeed."

Pugh sat back to consider his options. He didn't know what his options were yet but he hadn't been a Minister of three Government Departments without learning that there were options, there always were, there was always a way. It was finding it. One such way came to him more or less immediately. "Who knows about this? About them being contaminated?"

"Well Mr Wainwright. You and me of course. Mr Squelch...."

"Who's Mr Squelch when he's at home?"

"The Head of the Realistic Vaginal Juices Department. His real name is Quelch, but everybody.... And the operatives in Mr Squelch's department of course, they will know too because all their machines had to be decontaminated. A few of the office staff, they know."

"But the Africans? Do they know? Or the Government?"

"Well not so far as I'm aware. Mr Pugh told them there was a temporary glitch and that there would be a slight delay in fulfilling the order. We were about to start manufacturing replacements when the poor man died."

"But surely that didn't stop you? I mean you still had a huge order to fulfil."

"And just as soon as the factory had recovered from the tragedy of Mr Pugh's death we set about fulfilling it. But no sooner had we re-commenced production than the Realistic Vaginal Juices Department became contaminated again. We suspected foul play at first, but on investigation it turned out to be a deeply corroded inlet pipe. It set us back another two weeks while it was being replaced and we've only just got going again. And as I've already explained we've got way behind with customers' orders, they're turning to other manufacturers, several have cancelled, our creditors are banging on the door, and to top it off this afternoon I got no joy at all from the Inland Revenue and VAT people in my attempts to gain an extension to our already overdue obligations in that regard. So, like I say, An Hour In Bed isn't really worth a thing at the moment. We may in fact be losing money."

"Shit!"

"Indeed."

Plimmer sat back and folded his arms in the hope the gesture would indicate to Pugh that there was nothing more to be said about the matter. However something had dawned on Pugh. Something wasn't quite right, wasn't consistent with what he'd seen earlier in the day. He pointed it out. "But the factory is in full production."

"Yes. Producing and selling just about enough to service the interest payments on the loans we've already taken out to keep our heads above water, plus the loans we will have to take out in order to satisfy the demands of the Inland Revenue and the VAT people. I'm afraid we are in a vicious circle, Mr Pugh."

"So how much are we in the shit for?"

"How much do we owe?" Plimmer thought about it for a moment. "Ball Park, with the tax and Vat, about half a million pounds, give or take."

Pugh took in this latest bombshell and remained silent for a moment or two while he thought the situation through. Suddenly he cracked a smile as an idea suggested itself. Plimmer didn't like the look of it at all, neither the smile nor what such a smile might bode when it appeared on the face of what had already turned out to be a thoroughly obnoxious man. "So what's to stop us just sending them anyway?" Pugh finally said.

"Sending what?"

"The inflatable rubber women."

"To Africa?"

"No, fucking Timbuktu. Of course Africa, where else you moron?"

It passed through Plimmer's mind to inform Pugh that Timbuktu was in Africa. However a much more important thought pushed it out of the way. "But they're contaminated, Mr Pugh."

"Yes?"

"Well if someone were to have sex with one it would contaminate him."

"So? The buggers spend half the time scratching themselves anyway, what's a bit more scratching? Give them something to do."

Plimmer could scarcely believe his ears. He knew that

politicians could be quite ruthless in their dealings, and had even been known to start wars on a whim, but what Pugh was suggesting was quite monstrous. Fortunately his new boss wouldn't be able to go through with it. "The Foreign Minister knows," he said. "He was here, he knows the full story."

"Shit!"

"Indeed."

After lobbing back what he hoped was the final 'Indeed' in the Shit/Indeed rally, Plimmer went on: "Furthermore we're stuck with them until such time as the people from the Department of the Environment advise us what do with them."

"What? Why?"

"Well they're contaminated. We can't just dump them on the tip. Or burn them. We can't have thirty million poundsworth of contaminated inflatable rubber women polluting the atmosphere."

Pugh's jaw had dropped a few times during his meeting with Plimmer but now dropped to its lowest point yet. "Thirty million poundsworth?"

"That's just the costs of production of course. Forty five million if you include the profit element." Pugh's jaw almost reached the floor on hearing this. "Unfortunately they were from our de-luxe range, with realistic vaginal juices, so....."

Pugh blew his top. "Will you for Christ's sake stop going on about realistic vaginal juices!"

"I'm sorry. Familiarity you know. As far as we at An Hour In Bed are concerned we might just as well be talking about....oh, fruit gums or something."

"Well bloody well call them fruit gums in future when you're talking to me about them! Because I'm fed up to the back teeth with realistic vaginal juices!" The mental picture his words conjured up caused Pugh to clutch at his stomach in the anticipation it was going to turn over again.

Plimmer did his best to look concerned. "Are you all right, Mr Pugh?"

"All right? All fucking right? I come here under the impression I've inherited a profitable concern and you tell me I've inherited a pile of shit? No I am not all right, Plimmer, I am far from fucking all right!"

Plimmer shrugged. "Well I'm afraid that's the position Mr Pugh," he said, consolingly. "I wish it wasn't so, but...."

Utterly dejected Pugh got to his feet. "I'm going back to London."

*

Dejected as Pugh was he became even more dejected when on getting into his car a few minutes later he saw an inflatable rubber woman had been placed on the passenger seat. She was completely naked and there was a note stuck to her where her knickers would have been had she been wearing any. It read: 'Willing Wilma. With the compliments of a big fan of yours'.

"Of all the....!" Pugh was beside himself. As well as beside Willing Wilma. It wasn't very long before he realised that he might be beside her for quite some time.

Wishing to keep the news of his good fortune to himself for the time being Pugh had dispensed with the services of his chauffeur and had driven himself to Ramsbottom in his BMW Z4 sports coupe. Slaithwaite had a mouth on him and, whilst maybe not having the ear of the Prime Minister, had the ear of the Prime Minister's chauffeur, which was more than enough to make Pugh exercise caution.

The BMW was a very small car and Willing Wilma was a very big inflatable rubber woman, and although she may very well have been willing to supply sex on demand she proved to be totally unwilling to have herself removed from the car.

A complication was that Pugh didn't know whether she was one of the contaminated sex dolls or one of the new stock. Consequently he was forced to treat her as though she were the former. The problem this presented was exactly opposite to that faced by Elton Arbuckle when he was attempting to have sex with Bouncy Beyoncé, inasmuch as whilst Arbuckle was trying his hardest to get into the inflatable rubber woman Pugh was trying his hardest to keep out of it, or at least well away from the part of it that might contaminate him. This necessitated the battle being engaged at arm's length, and with the lack of leverage this strategy dictated it made an already difficult job almost impossible. After two minutes of Pugh's tugging and pushing in all directions Willing Wilma was no further from being removed from the car than when he'd started.

He had set about the task by getting out of the car, opening the passenger door and trying to pull her out by the breasts. Although her breasts had stretched far enough to start leaving the car the rest of her refused to follow. Pugh had therefore abandoned the method in favour of getting back into the driving seat and attempting to push her out, first with his arms, and, when this method bore no fruit, with his feet. Both to no avail. Although she was a different model than Bouncy Beyoncé, Willing Wilma shared Beyoncé's conical breasts, and a minute later, when attempting to wrestle Wilma out of the car, Pugh made his task even more difficult by poking himself in the eye with one of them.

Wiping his eye, he sat back to consider the problem. As if in sympathy Willing Wilma seemed to settle back in her seat. He thought to go for help, some manpower to drag the sex doll out of her new home, but the factory had closed at five thirty and it was now almost six. Damn Wainwright and Plimmer, they'd pay for this, by Christ would they.

He had one last attempt at jettisoning Wilma, during which he poked himself in his other eye with her other breast, then gave up the ghost. He would have to drive back to London with her in the passenger seat. He fervently hoped no one would see him, or her, especially her, but didn't much fancy his chances. The only thing going for him was that darkness was falling. Perhaps if he got his foot down it would help? Maybe if he was going fast Willing Wilma would be seen as just a blur and anyone seeing her might not recognise her as an inflatable rubber woman. Apart from that if he put his foot down it would get him home quicker, give people less time to see her anyway. He started the car and put his foot down.

Ten minutes into the journey he began to itch. Two seconds later itch's partner scratch joined the party. Pugh panicked. Christ, was Willing Wilma one of the contaminated rubber women? Had his skin become contaminated while he was trying to jettison her? Just thinking about it brought him out in a hot sweat. The hot sweat made him itch and scratch all the more. He had never itched so much in his life. He pulled in at the side of the road and scratched for England. Thankfully a few minutes later the itching began to subside, and with it the scratching. Five minutes later it stopped altogether. Pugh concluded that the attack must have been psychosomatic, that thinking about the contaminated inflatable rubber women must have brought it on. Fifteen minutes later, and with no further attacks of the itches, he was sure this had been the cause.

Two and a half hours later he was back home. Amazingly

no one had noticed the inflatable rubber woman at his side, not even when he'd passed through the brightly lit streets of London. Once, when he'd pulled up at traffic lights, the owner of the car that pulled up alongside him had looked directly at Willing Wilma, but had expressed no interest whatsoever. Pugh had decided that he was either short-sighted or a pervert who regularly took his own inflatable woman for a drive round, and had thought no more about it.

CHAPTER TWELVE

"Bless me Father, for I think I may have sinned."

Father Flannery smiled condescendingly. "To think about sin is as much a sin as the sin itself, my son."

"I didn't say I'd been thinking about sin," Father O'Riley replied, a little testily from the other side of the confessional box. "I said I think I may have sinned."

"You may have sinned?"

"I have done something I think might be a sin but I'm not sure if it is."

Flannery nodded wisely and settled back to listen. "You'd better tell me about it."

"I've had sex with an inflatable rubber woman."

Flannery had no doubts whatsoever and wasted no time in telling his fellow cleric. "I think we can safely say you have sinned, Father O' Riley."

"But in what way, Father Flannery? Granted, as a Roman Catholic priest I have taken a vow of celibacy. Which means I must not have sex with women." The priest paused, then added, his voice a mixture of doubt and hope, "But....?"

"But what?"

"Women, Father Flannery. I must not have sex with women. Women, with flesh and blood. And I didn't have sex with a real flesh and blood woman, did I? Merely a lump of rubber. When you look at it in that way it's little more than masturbating. In fact it was just like masturbating, despite what it said on the box about it being the ultimate carnal experience. And we all masturbate now and then don't we."

"Yes, of course, but....no, no we most certainly do not all

masturbate now and then, Father O'Riley!" said Flannery, instantly feeling hot under the collar.

O'Riley smiled knowingly. "No, of course we don't, Father Flannery."

"And furthermore, might I say Father O'Riley, having sex with an inflatable rubber woman is a little bit more than masturbating. Condoms don't have breasts and other womanly things, at least not any condoms I've ever come into contact with. Not that I've come into contact with any," he added quickly. He shook his head. "I'm not even sure you should be masturbating in a condom. A condom is a method of birth control and I'm sure you don't need me to tell you of the Catholic Church's doctrine in regard to that. Ten *Hail Mary's* and ten *Our Fathers*."

When he had made his judgement Father Flannery had not the slightest doubt that he'd come to the right decision; certainly from a theological and moral viewpoint. However later that evening, relaxing with a glass of red wine, he began to have doubts. *Was* having sex with an inflatable rubber woman the same as having sex with a real woman? In deed, if not in fact? It was something he had never thought about, had never had to think about. He thought about it now.

Father O'Riley's admission had taken him completely by surprise. Had the enormity of it, the nature of it, caught him off balance, forced him into making a hasty decision? He dwelled on it for a minute or so before shrugging it off as so much nonsense. Of course it hadn't. Of course having sex with an inflatable rubber woman was wrong, very wrong, what on earth was he thinking about, considering for even one moment that it wasn't wrong.

He poured himself a second glass of wine, put aside the Harry Potter that the patient he had visited in the lunatic asylum had recommended, and settled down with the Bible to look for suitable questions for the next quiz night at *The Grim Jogger*.

It had been an excellent idea of his to volunteer to set the questions for the weekly quiz, following the death of the last setter from an aneurysm, which ironically had been the answer to one of the last questions he'd ever asked. The type of questions posed had been given a complete make-over, and while about half of them were still secular the remainder were now about religion in general and the Holy Bible in particular. Questions about the Good Book would be a perfect way to get the members of the quiz teams interested in reading it, and would be far more beneficial than all the usual questions about football and pop stars and television shows. True, the number of teams taking part in the quiz had dropped from an average of fifteen to an average of eight since he'd taken over setting the questions, but then not everyone liked answering questions on the Bible, he understood that. But equally true, there were lots of people out there who would enjoy answering questions on the Bible, given the opportunity, and they would be bound to come along to *The Grim Jogger* as soon as news of the new quiz format had got around.

A third truth was that there was a certain ignorance of biblical knowledge exhibited by those teams who still took part. For example when he had posed the question 'Who was Moses?' a third of the participants, possibly expecting a question about films, had answered 'Charlton Heston'. But he was sure it was only because they were on a learning curve and it would be only a matter of time before they got used to the new format.

Remembering to forego questions about the Madonna -

there had been the most unholy row about her at the last quiz night when one of the quizzers had tried to claim that the Holy Mother was an American pop star - he settled to his task. He had just set another question involving Moses: 'Subtract the days Jesus spent on the cross from the days Moses spent in the wilderness and divide by the Commandment which mentions graven images', and was working on another one about Samson. However he was finding it difficult to concentrate as doubts about whether having sex with an inflatable rubber woman was or wasn't a sin began to enter his head again, the thought of graven images possibly having triggered it off. And the more he thought about it the more doubtful he became. For what harm was there in having intercourse with a sex doll? Really? It would be different if you had sex with a real woman, a flesh and blood woman as Father O'Riley had put it; that would be a different thing altogether, for the moment you had sex with a real woman you had obligations towards that woman, and that's where the trouble started. But what obligations had you towards a piece of rubber? None. You couldn't harm a piece of rubber.

By the time Flannery had finished his third glass of wine he was even more doubtful. Where in the Bible did it say that Roman Catholic priests shouldn't have sex with inflatable rubber women? It didn't. If it had he would have already set it as a question in the pub quiz. Where in the Bible did it even mention inflatable rubber women? Not in any book of the Bible he'd ever read, not in the New Testament, not in the Old; not even in Revelations, and what a revelation that would have been if they had been mentioned! But they hadn't.

After drinking a fourth glass of wine he was so convinced he'd come to the wrong decision that he phoned Fr O'Riley to cut his penance down to three Hail Mary's and two Our Fathers. It took quite a time for O'Riley to come to the phone as he was having sex with his inflatable rubber woman at the time, but eventually he came and he came. O'Riley thanked him very much but said he needn't have bothered because he wasn't going to recite the Hail Marys and the Our Fathers anyway as he thought Flannery had been wrong in his judgement. After a fifth glass of wine Flannery totally agreed with him. And by the time he'd finished the bottle he was on the internet looking for suppliers of inflatable rubber women.

That had been two weeks ago. The inflatable rubber woman, courtesy of An Hour In Bed, had arrived a week later. After taking Religious Rita out of the package his inclination had been to send her back immediately and ask for her to be replaced with Sexy Susie or one of the other sex dolls. Having sex with an inflatable rubber woman was one thing, having carnal knowledge of one dressed as a nun was quite another, and he wondered what on earth he must have been thinking about when he'd sent off for her. Possibly it was a nagging doubt that he still might have been wrong in his decision to go down the Fr O'Riley path, and doing it with a religious personage might make him just that bit less guilty of mortal sin. But that apart, he'd had plenty of time to think about it by now. His thoughts had convinced him that maybe it hadn't been the best idea he'd ever had.

Acting on these thoughts, before darker thoughts returned to elbow the pure thoughts out of the way again, he parcelled up Religious Rita with the intention of sending her back first thing in the morning. However another bottle of Chateau Communion Wine that evening interfered with his plans. By the fourth glass he'd got back to thinking what possible harm there could be in having sex with an inflatable woman, after the fifth glass he'd unpackaged her again, and by the time he'd emptied the bottle he was in bed with Religious Rita, had had sex with her and was seriously thinking about having it again.

Having it again was the last thing he was thinking about after he awoke the following morning with her beside him; thinking about the first time he'd had it with her was bad enough. Mercifully he couldn't see her face, but only because it was still covered by her habit, which he had hoisted up over her head the night before as he hadn't liked the idea of her looking at him while he was having sex with her.

He was immediately overcome with a dreadful remorse. What in God's name had he done! He had fallen by the wayside. Fallen just as surely as the fallen women he daily admonished and handed out Hail Marys and Our Fathers to when they came to him to confess their sins. Fallen just as surely as the fornicating men who had caused the fallen women to fall in the first place. Damn Religious Rita! Damn An Hour In Bed! He wished he'd never heard of them.

Suddenly he knew what he must do, what action he must take that would at least go some way to absolving himself from the terrible sin he'd visited upon himself. Atonement! He must make atonement. Sackcloth and ashes. Self-inflicted punishment would get him off the slippery slope and back onto the straight and narrow. A spell in purgatory, that was the remedy, that was the way out of the sinful pit he'd allowed himself to slide into.

But what form would his penance take? Not Hail Marys and Our Fathers. He'd be reciting Hail Marys and Our Fathers for ever more if he were to recite enough of them to purge himself of such a terrible sin. Not flagellation either, he'd tried that the last time he'd masturbated and had had to stop when he'd started enjoying it more than the masturbation. He would have to stigmatize himself. Nothing short of that would be enough to purge him. Maim himself, that would do the trick. He would wear a suit made of spikes like that priest in *The Da Vinci Code*. An action as extreme as that would be bound to cleanse him.

He sincerely hoped he wouldn't enjoy it, like he had the flagellation, otherwise he didn't know what he'd do.

CHAPTER THIRTEEN

On his return from the visit to An Hour In Bed Hugh Pugh, tired and weary from his journey, all the scratching, and his exertions in unsuccessfully jettisoning Willing Wilma from his car, had informed Lorelei that he was having an early night and had gone straight to bed. To Lorelei's surprise he was snoring his head off when she followed him a few minutes later; usually when he mentioned an early night he had a pre-slumbers bout of torrid sex in mind.

At just turned three-o-clock in the morning Pugh suddenly awoke, sweating profusely. Every part of his body was itching like mad. It was just like the itching he'd experienced on the drive back to London but about ten times worse. He knew the cause of it immediately. He'd been contaminated by that blasted inflatable rubber woman. Whether or not the itching he'd had before had been psychosomatic or a precursor of the real itching to come he didn't know. What he did know was that something would have to be done about it, and pretty quick, before he scratched himself away.

He sat up in bed, switched on the bedside light and roughly shook Lorelei awake. She turned to him, rubbed her eyes and looked sleepily at the clock.

"What have we got for itching?" Pugh asked, feverishly scratching his chest with one hand and his scrotum with the other.

"Christ Almighty, Pughie, it's three-o-clock in the morning!" Lorelei complained.

"Never mind that, I'm scratching myself to death here," said Pugh, scratching himself to death. "Have we got anything for it?"

"Itching?" Lorelei thought for a moment. "Well I've got some of that stuff the doctor gave me when I had thrush; that might help."

Pugh changed the target areas of his scratching from his chest and his scrotum to the back of his neck and his feet, then quickly moved on to his buttocks and knees before switching back to his chest and scrotum, which had immediately started itching again the moment he'd stopped scratching them. Lorelei pulled a face and edged back a little from him as though she'd just found out he was a leper or a *Big Issue* seller. "Bloody hell, Pughie," she said, "where you been?"

"Never mind that, just get me that cunt cream and bloody quick about it."

Muttering complainingly, Lorelei got out of bed and made her way to the bathroom. Still itching furiously, Pugh scratched on, his hands darting about all over his body, scratching here, scratching there, homing in on one part of his body then moving on to another part before he'd hardly had time to scratch the part he'd moved to.

Between scratches he managed to tear off his pyjamas. He caught a glimpse of himself in the large mirror on the wall which matched the ones on the other three walls and the ceiling. He gasped at the sight. The five reflected Pughs were covered from head to foot in red blotches. Angry purple wheals, where he'd scratched himself, stood out against the few parts of him that what were still pink, and he was bleeding in several places where his fingernails had dug into to his podgy flesh. The removal of his pyjamas had made the itches easier to get at; whether that was a good thing or not was debateable as scratching them might make matters worse than they already were.

Hadn't he read somewhere that cold helped with itching? Maybe if he immersed himself in a bath of very cold water it would stop it? Some ice cubes in it would help. But he wouldn't be able to immerse his head, if he immersed his head he would drown, and his head was itching as much as the rest of him was itching. How would he be able to scratch it if his hands were underwater? He decided that his head would just have to itch if it meant the rest of his body was itching a bit less, and was about to shout to Lorelei to tell her to start running a cold bath and check for ice cubes when she returned from the bathroom with the thrush ointment.

"I've found one or two other things you can try as well," she said, putting jars and tubes down on the dressing table top. Pugh was still scratching like there was no tomorrow but if there was a tomorrow he'd still be scratching when it arrived. "If you can stop scratching for long enough for me to put them on you," she continued. She pointed to them in turn, a stallholder offering her wares. "I've got the stuff the doctor gave me for thrush, some lanoline - that's good for itching I think - some anti-histamine ointment, and some Calamine lotion I got when I got sunburned that time on that fact-finding mission; it's very good for itching as well, Calamine lotion, I remember from that time I had hives. Which one do you want to try?"

"All of them, put the bloody lot on," said Pugh desperately.

Lorelei was unsure. "Oh I don't think that's a good idea, Pughie; I mean you never know what might happen, I mean they might react with each other or something."

"I'll react by giving you a belt round the earhole if you don't stop fucking about and get something on me," snarled

Pugh, attacking an already bleeding part of his anatomy anew. "Ouch!"

Lorelei bridled. "You oughtn't to be talking to me like that, Pughie. I *am* an ex-WAG you know."

"You'll be an ex-fucking girlfriend if you don't move your arse and get on with it. So let's have some action, shall we!"

Lorelei considered the situation for a moment. "I tell you what I'll do. I'll split you into quarters. I'll do a quarter of you with the lanoline, a quarter with the anti-histamine, a quarter with the Calamine lotion and a quarter with the thrush stuff. Then whichever works best for you I'll do you all over with it."

Pugh felt like splitting Lorelei into quarters and doing her all over if it would only make her shut up yapping and get on with it, but he simply nodded his agreement. Lorelei set to work and a few minutes later Pugh, lanolined, anti-histamined, Calamined and thrushed, stood and waited for the various sprays and lotions to take effect.

Lorelei, mindful of her warning that there might be a bad reaction if one or more of the assorted lotions happened to get mixed up with each other, had artfully allowed them to overlap at the approximate centre of the four quadrants of Pugh, namely his genital area, in the hope that she might cause a bit of damage there and pay him back for being so horrid to her.

All the various treatments helped to abate the itching to some degree, especially in the genital area, which rather worryingly for Pugh had gone completely numb. Even so he still itched quite a bit and it was all he could do to stop himself from scratching. The best of the treatments turned out to be the Calamine lotion. Having established this Lorelei got Pugh to shower, in order to remove all the other anti-scratching aids.

Having provided herself with a clean canvas on which to paint, Lorelei then set to work with the Calamine lotion. After she had covered Pugh from head to foot in the bright pink liquid she stood back to admire her handiwork.

"You look just like an inflatable rubber man," she said. "If there are such things."

Pugh was to wonder the same thing himself before very much longer.

CHAPTER FOURTEEN

Yet another man to rue the appearance of an inflatable rubber woman in his life was George Grimshaw, for it was one such that was indirectly responsible for his being summarily dismissed from his job as a postman.

About six months previously Grimshaw had been happily treading the streets in the course of his duties. Grimshaw loved his job, it kept him fit and got him out in the open air. He liked the simple, uncomplicated nature of a postman's job. It wasn't quite as uncomplicated as his wife had tried to make out - when he'd first got the job and mentioned to her that he had to attend a training course before being sent out on his first round she'd said "A training course to learn how to walk? I've been able to walk since I was one" - but it wasn't so complicated as to occupy one's mind overmuch. Just as long as you remembered little things like not putting your hand through the letter box along with the letter, especially when the space immediately behind the door might be occupied by a particularly vicious dog, your mind could go wherever it wanted to go; it was only your legs that the Royal Mail required.

However Grimshaw's job began to get much more complicated the day he noticed that a parcel he was about to deliver, to one of the more up-market houses on his route, had a corner ripped off. The postman, a naturally inquisitive man who made a habit of reading postcards sent from holidaymakers to their friends and loved ones, could not resist a peep inside. After making the hole a bit bigger he found that the parcel contained a sex toy. He didn't realise it was a sex toy at first; it looked for all the world like a brightly-coloured plastic toy gun, something a little boy might use to shoot baddies when he was imagining he was Luke Skywalker or Indiana Jones. It was only on closer examination – and after turning the parcel upside down and shaking it, whereupon the contents fell out onto the pavement – that he realised it was a 'LoveHoney 7 Function Vibrating Cock Ring 2.0.' (as it stated on the box).

It was at this point that Grimshaw began to have grave doubts about his chosen profession. From being a man who simply delivered letters and parcels to people's homes he now realised that he was also a courier of sex toys, an inadvertent provider of porn. He was outraged.

Grimshaw had never enjoyed sex – he had only ever had it with his wife, who had always given a fair imitation of a log whilst grudgingly supplying it, and nowadays didn't supply it at all. Deprived of enjoyable sex himself he didn't like other people enjoying it, which they obviously did, for it was all over the place, you couldn't move without being aware of it; in the papers - 'CHERYL'S NEW LOVER'; on the telly – *"There are scenes of a sexual nature"*; in the pub – *"What you looking so pleased with yourself about Dave, get your end away last night? Got a promise? Jesus look at the tits on that new barmaid, I could shag that!"* The whole world was at it.

From that day on every parcel wrapped in plain brown paper had been treated by Grimshaw with a deep suspicion, looked at with narrowed eyes, poked at by his index finger, squeezed by his hands, held to his ear and rattled, all in an effort to determine the contents inside. Anything cylindrical and between six inches and a foot long was treated with particular distrust. Despite his deepest suspicions, and notwithstanding all the looking with narrowed eyes and poking and squeezing and rattling, Grimshaw could never be one hundred per cent sure that any of the suspect packages which emerged with monotonous regularity from the depths of his postbag actually contained sex toys. But one thing he was absolutely sure about was that if he ever did manage to discover a sex toy it certainly wouldn't be going through the letter box or handed over the doorstep to the pervert who'd sent for it. It would be thrown without delay and without ceremony on the council tip. Two completely innocent rolling pins had already received this fate.

Shortly after the incident with the LoveHoney 7 Function Vibrating Cock Ring 2.0. Grimshaw saw an advert in the local freebie newspaper - '*Vigilantes Against Sex Toys, come and join us*'. He had needed no further invitation. A little sceptical at first - he suspected from the invitation to 'come and join us' that Vigilantes Against Sex Toys might be a front for the Salvation Army who were having a recruiting drive - he had gone along to the next meeting. He arrived there to discover his fears were completely unfounded. There was no sign of any tambourines, far less a big drum or euphonium. And although the members of VAST were as zealous in their belief as even the staunchest followers of William Booth, their zeal manifested itself not in the dishing out of bowlfuls of soup and hope to the needy but to targeting purveyors of sex toys. Grimshaw was made up.

After the meeting had ended and all the members of VAST had gone their separate ways, save for Willoughby, Grimshaw had discussed his dilemma with VAST's chairman. The society's leading light had promised to give the matter some thought. By the time the next meeting came round he had come up with an idea which he thought might go a long way to solving Grimshaw's problem. VAST would purchase, for the exclusive use of Grimshaw whilst doing his postman's round, an X-Ray machine. This apparatus would enable him to scan suspicious-looking packages and weed out and discard the ones that satisfied his suspicions. "And will fail to satisfy the perverts who had been expecting them," Willoughby had said, in a rare attempt at humour.

In the two months since Grimshaw had been provided with the X-ray machine he had weeded out and discarded no less than twelve such items, plus a baby's novelty potty that looked suspiciously like the 'LoveHoney Sqweel Oral Sex Simulator' he had weeded out the week before, along with another rolling pin which he had weeded out by mistake and couldn't get back into the package.

It was the fifteenth item he discovered that proved to be his undoing. It was Glorious Gloria, one of An Hour In Bed's inflatable rubber women. There had been no need to open it, the X-ray machine had clearly revealed the contents. Grimshaw had continued on his round, Glorious Gloria stowed safely in his postbag, never to be stowed safely in the loft away from the prying eyes off Mrs Donaldson, whose husband had ordered the offending and offensive article.

Before embarking on his part-time career as keeper of the public's morals Grimshaw had considered the possibility that his activities might one day be discovered. He had come to the decision that it wasn't likely. His reasoning was that customers, on failing to receive a sex toy they had ordered, were hardly likely to complain to the Royal Mail about it. The sheer embarrassment it would cause them would see to that.

And he was probably right. But what he didn't take into account was that a customer who failed to take delivery of a sex toy he'd ordered might complain to the suppliers from whom he'd ordered it. Which all the customers did.

After a few such complaints an investigation was mounted by the Royal Mail authorities and suspicion fell on Grimshaw. An official from their head office special security team was detailed to tail the errant postman in order to prove or disprove their suspicions.

On the third day of being tailed Grimshaw's X-ray machine had revealed that the large parcel headed for one Dr Arthur Snood almost certainly contained an inflatable rubber woman. He couldn't be absolutely sure; there was a chance it could be a pink blow up plastic pouffe.

This had been the case a couple of weeks previously, as when both items were folded up flat they looked very similar (although perhaps a more observant person than Grimshaw might have noted that pouffes don't usually wear G-strings). On that occasion, when he had taken the package to the tip and opened it up in order to confirm his suspicions, he had been disappointed to discover it contained nothing but the pouffe. However before he could re-package it a flock of gulls had swooped down on it, no doubt thinking it was food, and had pecked a thousand holes in it before discovering their mistake.

Grimshaw, having learned his lesson, now chose a spot on the tip well away from where the gulls were currently foraging. He ripped away the brown paper and opened the cardboard box inside. Just as he suspected it contained an inflatable rubber woman, along with a card, tastefully tucked down the elastic waistband of her black lace thong. Written on the card in a graceful gold-coloured longhand script were the words '*Glorious Gloria. With the compliments of An Hour In Bed. Enjoy.*'

On the three previous occasions Grimshaw had discovered sex dolls in his postbag he had simply dumped them on the tip. However this time, mindful of Farzad Khan's s eldest son getting his hand stuck in the wankee-doodle-dandy, and fearful of what the Afghan's offspring might get stuck in an inflatable rubber woman should he chance upon it, Grimshaw's plan was to destroy it. He thought he might accomplish this by walking over to where the gulls were scavenging and simply tossing it to them so they could peck a thousand holes in it as they had the pouffe. However when he looked over to where they were flocking, some hundred yards or so away, he spotted a man nearby. Not wishing to draw attention to himself he was forced to revise his plan.

To carry out his strategy he now took out his penknife with the idea of stabbing a few holes in the inflatable rubber woman, thus rendering it Farzad Khan's-eldest-son-proof. Unfortunately his first stab scored a direct hit on Glorious Gloria's valve. It was enough for her to suddenly start inflating. Thankfully, unlike the occasion when Arbuckle's rubber woman had suddenly inflated, Glorious Gloria stopped inflating when she reached her normal size. Even so she presented a fearsome sight; a pink medley of arms, legs, breasts and buttocks, topped by a grotesque long blonde-haired head, her face set in a gruesome grin.

Grimshaw shuddered at the sight of it. He pulled himself together. This wasn't getting the baby bathed. Or Glorious Gloria dealt with. But what to do? He looked all around him to see if there was anyone about. Just the man by the gulls. But the man was on the move now, and heading towards him. Shit! He thought quickly. The best course of action seemed to be to continue with his original plan to stab holes in the inflatable rubber woman and make himself scarce before the man started asking awkward questions. However it didn't help matters that he was still in his postman's uniform and there was clear evidence that a parcel had been opened.

With not a second to waste he set about puncturing Glorious Gloria. This proved to be easier said than done. Glorious Gloria was one of An Hour In Bed's de-luxe range and as such was 'made of specially toughened and puncture-proof rubber for year upon year of satisfyingly sexy nights'. Whether the puncture-proof rubber would have withstood the attentions of a tungsten carbide-tipped electric drill is debateable but it certainly proved to be tough enough to prevent Grimshaw's Woolworth's penknife penetrating it. Twelve times he plunged the penknife into Glorious Gloria and twelve times it bounced back off her toughened de-luxe hide.

He looked around for something sharper. He spotted a discarded old metal car bumper bar a few yards away. It looked pretty solid, heavy, and with luck would have sharp edges. Surely if he threw that down on her with enough force it would pop her? He went to get it, but on the way struck gold. An old companion set, complete with a poker, had been thrown away. Just the thing. He noticed that the end of the poker, obviously having done a lot of poking, was worn to a point. Excellent. He made his way back to Glorious Gloria, dropped to his knees beside her, raised his arm high over his head and prepared to plunge the poker into to her.

It was at that point that the weather decided to take a hand. A gentle breeze is often called 'playful', but as far as Grimshaw was concerned there was nothing playful about the gentle breeze that now suddenly appeared from nowhere and lifted Glorious Gloria off the ground. She was four feet above the rubbish tip and rising before the startled postman pulled himself together enough to make a grab for her. Having snatched hold of her he wrestled her to the ground, then lay on top of her to keep her from becoming airborne again while he thought things through. It was clear to him that once he let go of her she would probably be off on her travels again before he'd had the chance to pop her. While he was still thinking about how he could overcome this latest snag the man who had been making his way over from the gulls, Mr Jennison of the Royal Mail Security Team, arrived on the scene. He stopped at Grimshaw, looked down on him and coughed discreetly to gain his attention. Grimshaw turned to him, surprised and aghast.

"And what do you think you're up to?" said Jennison, arching his eyebrows.

If Grimshaw had been given a week in which to think of a suitable answer he may possibly have arrived at something believable. At such short notice the only excuses he could come up with were that he had suspected a package in his mailbag had contained a bomb, whereupon he had opened it and discovered what he took to be a large quantity of pink plastic explosive disguised as an inflatable rubber woman, which he was now trying to de-fuse. Alternatively, he was practising for his forthcoming holiday on which, as a devout sun-worshipper, he intended to spend the whole two weeks lying on a lilo. He decided that neither excuse sounded convincing, so he said, rather lamely: "This isn't as bad as it looks."

"Well it looks like you've been tampering with the Royal Mail," said Jennison, "And that having tampered with it you are now shagging the arse off the contents of it; how much worse can it look?"

Within the hour Grimshaw had been paid off and sacked.

CHAPTER FIFTEEN

"Balance of his mind disturbed?" said Dr Featherstone, doubtfully.

Pugh attempted to laugh off the doctor's doubts. It wasn't doubts he was looking for, doubts didn't get you out of the shit. "Well it's obvious," he said. "The man gave away ten million pounds; you'd have to be stark raving mad to do that."

Dr Featherstone shook his head. "Not really. Men have given away far larger amounts. Getty, Carnegie, more recently Bill Gates, a whole host of philanthropically-minded people."

"And did these philanthropically-minded people also have themselves buried in a woman's fanny?"

The doctor almost choked on the last of his roast widgeon with blackcurrant jus. "Pardon?"

"Because my brother Aneurin did," said Pugh, peeved. "And if that isn't the action of somebody who's as mad as a bloody hatter I don't know what is."

Pugh had spent two days embalmed in the Calamine lotion whilst waiting for the itching to abate. By then it had set to a consistency of plaster of Paris. When he finally emerged from his suit of pink armour it was not without considerable pain. Refusing point blank to immerse himself in a hot bath or take a shower in order to break down and melt the Calamine, fearful that the hot water would set him off itching again, he had instructed Lorelei to chip it off with a blunt knife. As Pugh was by no means short of body hair, which by this time the Calamine had taken an iron grip on, this was by no means a straightforward procedure. Pugh was particularly hirsute in the chest and groin area, and it was on these parts of his body that not insubstantial pieces of him came away along with the Calamine and the hair. By the time Lorelei had completed her work his chest had only slightly more hair than a billiard ball.

After she had made several attempts at freeing the Calamine from his genitals, to screams of pain from Pugh, he had opted to leave things as they were down there and allow it to wear off in the fullness of time. Lorelei had told him that there was no way she was having sex with him while his penis was bigger and harder than usual, because it was quite big and hard enough as it already was. Pugh decided that they would cross that bridge when they came to it.

The bridge was in danger of having to be crossed much sooner than he expected, when, on passing the time before bedtime by tuning in to his usual porn channel, he had obtained an erection. However his tumescence immediately caused small lumps of dried Calamine lotion to try to tear themselves from his genitals. The excruciating pain this brought with it rendered his penis instantly limp again and he abandoned all thoughts of sex and switched over to *Meet Vanessa Feltz* so it wouldn't happen again.

Whilst entombed in the Calamine Pugh had had time to think, to contemplate the state of affairs he had been placed in *viz a viz* his inheritance, and to deliberate on how he could turn the situation to his advantage. Several avenues that might prove fruitful had suggested themselves. Trying to prove that his brother gave away the ten million pounds while the balance of his mind was disturbed was the second of the avenues he explored, hence the expensive lunch at the *Waterside Inn* at Bray with his psychiatrist, Dr Featherstone.

Pugh had first availed himself of Dr Featherstone's

services following the nervous breakdown he'd suffered on learning how much alimony the judge had awarded his first wife following their divorce, and had used him ever since. The psychiatrist had been particularly helpful at the time of the MP's expenses scandal.

"Well it is rather odd, I must admit," Featherstone said, after Pugh had filled him in with the details of Aneurin's coffin requirements. "But I would tend to say it was the action of someone who is perhaps a trifle eccentric, even...."

It was Pugh's turn to almost choke on his food. "A trifle eccentric? Having yourself buried in a woman's fanny?"

"....even bizarre," Featherstone continued, "rather than the behaviour of a man who is no longer in control of his senses. I'm pretty sure that expert opinion would concur."

Pugh glowered. "So you don't think it's on then?"

"I'm afraid not." He looked at his empty plate. "Are we having a sweet?"

Featherstone did not get his sweet, and it was all Pugh could do to foot the bill for what the doctor had already eaten.

The first idea Pugh had come up with, a quite obvious one to a man of Pugh's inherent trickiness, was to have a fire. A good-old fashioned drop of arson was often the solution to a lot of problems. It had already been the answer to the problem of the thatched roof of a cottage he'd once had in the Cotswolds. Along with a serious dry rot problem the property would have cost almost as much to repair as it was worth. It had consequently gone up in smoke, thanks to a judiciously knocked over oil lamp that Pugh had blamed on the cat.

However his hand mustn't be seen to be on it if the inflatable rubber woman factory were to go up in flames. This wasn't four hundred grand for a country cottage we were talking about here, this was millions. The stock of inflatable rubber women alone was worth thirty million at cost, according to Plimmer. For this sort of job a third party would have to be used. A man skilled in the art of arson.

Fortunately he knew such a man; reliable, discreet, an ex-Fire Chief now at the Department of Energy and Climate Change. A phone call was made to arrange a change of climate in and around the An Hour In Bed factory, a fee agreed (£10,000 and for that there won't even be cinders to sift through never mind any evidence of foul play, the ex-Fire Chief had said), a time arranged (the following night, the sooner the better), and it was a done job. A second phone call was made, this time to Plimmer, to find out how much the payout from the insurance would be. Finally a third call was made, to the ex-Fire Chief again, to cancel the fire, after he'd learned from Plimmer that An Hour In Bed didn't have any fire insurance - they hadn't been able to afford to pay the premium when it had come up for renewal due to the financial situation at the factory.

On returning to his office the increasingly worried Pugh had explored the third avenue that might get him out of the position he'd been landed in; the possibility of a refund of some of the ten million pounds that Aneurin had given to Cleek University. A call was made to the Vice-Chancellor.

"Hugh Pugh here, Vice-Chancellor," he said, on being put through. "Secretary of State for Transport," he added, in case the academic hadn't heard of him, very likely in his opinion, university wallahs living with their heads in the clouds as they did. "I believe you knew my brother Aneurin?"

"Oh indeed, Mr Pugh, indeed."

"Are you aware that he recently passed away?"

"Most sad. Most sad indeed. He was a great man, a great benefactor. The university was about to offer him an honorary doctorate when he passed. Services to the entertainment industry."

Pugh wondered fleetingly if the proposed doctorate might be offered to him instead, in view of what he was about to do for the university. He quite fancied being called Dr Pugh. He'd mention it if things went to plan. He continued: "I'm calling about the ten million pounds he gave to your university."

"Yes?"

"You will no doubt be pleased to learn that as the only beneficiary in Aneurin's will I will be carrying on with his financial support of Cleek University."

The Vice-Chancellor was both surprised and delighted on hearing this news. "Really?"

"Each and every year, starting next year, I will be writing you a cheque for the sum of two million pounds."

The Vice-Chancellor was overcome. "This is most generous of you, Mr Pugh. This is magnificent news, quite magnificent."

"It is only what my brother would have wanted."

"Your brother was a very generous man, Mr Pugh. And you too are a very generous man, if I may say so."

"You may." The prospective Dr Pugh paused before going on. "There's just one small thing."

"Yes?"

"I find that the ten million pounds he gave you had the unfortunate effect of leaving An Hour In Bed with a slight cash flow problem. Nothing to worry about, just a temporary thing. But to cover it - to help An Hour In Bed out with in the generous way in which my brother helped you out, and that I will be helping you out in the future - I would like you to loan a million pounds of it back to me."

The line went quiet for a moment. "Loan you a million pounds?" the Vice-Chancellor eventually replied, as if he couldn't quite believe what Pugh had said.

"Just for a couple of months, until the cash flow problem is resolved."

This time the Vice-Chancellor's reply was immediate. "Well I would love to of course, Mr Pugh. But unfortunately all the money has been allocated. Spent indeed. Setting up the new Sex and Inflatable Rubber Woman Studies Department. And the new...."

Pugh never found out what the other new thing the university had spent the ten million pounds on as he slammed the phone down on the Vice-Chancellor.

A further attempt to gain from his inheritance was made with a phone call to the United States.

"Am I speaking to Claude C Greenbaum, the president of Molls Unlimited?"

"You are indeed. What can I do for you, Mr Pugh?"

"I am the owner of An Hour In Bed. You may have heard of us?" Pugh said, confident that the American would be aware of the British equivalent of Molls Unlimited.

"Can't say I have. An Hour In Bed, you say? What's your line, bed linen maybe?"

Pugh sighed. It might prove to be a bit more difficult than he'd imagined. "We are Britain's largest manufacturer of inflatable rubber women."

"Really? We have that same honour on our side of the pond. Last year we supplied over one million happy Americans with our love dolls. That's a helluva lot of humping every which way you look at it."

Pugh preferred not to look at it at all. By now even the thought of one inflatable rubber woman was beginning to sicken him, let alone the thought of Americans having sex with a million of them. In case Greenbaum had plans to enlighten him further about the sex habits of America's male population he cut immediately to the chase. "I won't beat about the bush, Mr Greenbaum, I...."

"Why not, that's just what made the one million happy Americans happy," said Greenbaum, with a laugh.

"Fuck me, what have I landed myself with here," said Pugh, under his breath. He gritted his teeth and ploughed on. "As I was saying, I'll come right to the point. I've got terminal cancer."

The line went quiet for a moment. When Greenbaum spoke again the flippancy had been replaced with polite respect. "Aw gee whizz. That's real tough. Is there anything I can do to help?"

Pugh crossed his fingers and took a deep breath. "Yes, there is as a matter of fact. You see I've no one to leave my business to so I'm putting it up for sale, giving the proceeds to charity. I can let you have the lot, lock stock and barrel, for five million pounds. And that includes one million inflatable rubber women," he said, then added, temptingly, "Which could make your one million happy Americans even happier than they already are."

"Well that's very generous of you, Mr Pugh, I'm sure. But unfortunately we're not thinking in term of adding to our overseas interests ever since the Greenland fiasco. So I'm afraid it's got to be a no no."

Despite his disappointment Pugh was intrigued. "What Greenland fiasco?"

"We opened a plant there. Imagined we'd do big love doll

business. And why not? All that cold, a guy's gotta do something to keep warm, and what better way to do it than humping? Thought the Eskimos would go for them in a big way. I mean have you seen those Eskimo women? Fat, and all that fur and all. Must be like humping a bear. Maybe worse. I know which I'd prefer to hump and it don't speak Eskimo."

"They didn't sell?"

"Oh they sold all right. At first. Damned Eskimos kept getting stuck to them."

"Stuck?"

"Yes, they'd hump the ass off the love dolls then drop off to sleep while they were still aboard. Then the sweat they'd worked up by humping them froze and they'd wake up frozen to them. They had to chip themselves off before they could go out fishing, or whatever else they do to pull in a dollar over there. Well word got round and sales stopped dead, just like that."

Pugh dropped the price of An Hour In Bed down to four million pounds, then three, then two, and finally one, before giving up on the American.

He then took stock of the situation. He was disappointed that none of his three ideas had worked - he expected at least one of them would have hit the jackpot - but far from downhearted. He hadn't aired his best idea yet. His banker. The implementation of it wouldn't be exactly cut and dried but he was sure he could put forward a very convincing case for it. He would have gone for it first, and not even bothered with the others, but when he'd phoned the Foreign Secretary earlier he'd been out of the office. He tried him again and this time got his man.

"Yes what can I do for you, Hugh?" he said.

"John. Nice to speak to you again."

"Likewise."

"Vera keeping well? And the children?"

"It's Hortense now."

"Shit." Pugh had heard that the Foreign Secretary had divorced and remarried but had completely forgotten about it.

"Pardon?"

Pugh quickly recovered from his gaffe. "Hortense! But of course it is. Me and my memory. Not getting any younger, John." Back on course again he got down to business. "John it's about these one million inflatable rubber women we were going to send to Africa, before they got contaminated."

"How did you know about that?"

"Westminster, John. You can't stop people talking. The thing is, I think we should send them to Africa anyway."

"Quite out of the question. As you yourself have just said, they're all contaminated."

It was the response Pugh had expected. Having thought the whole thing through, and answered every possible objection, he was ready for it. "Right. But, and correct me if I'm wrong John, the Africans won't use the condoms we already send them. Which is the reason we were sending them the inflatable rubber women. So what's going to happen now? I'll tell you. They're going to carry on having unprotected sex. And we all know how that's going to end up. More babies. So we send them the contaminated inflatable rubber women. Result, no more babies. All right, they'll all be scratching their bollocks off, but at least they won't be making babies and costing us a small fortune in foreign aid. And even if they scratch themselves to death it won't make a great deal of difference because most of the buggers are going to die from Aids or starvation anyway. I mean by sending them the contaminated inflatable rubber women we'll be doing them a favour in a way."

The line went quiet for a few seconds. Then the Foreign Secretary spoke. "You are aware that Hortense is African are you, Hugh?"

CHAPTER SIXTEEN

Mrs Wisbech had invited Mrs Bean and Miss Preece to her house ostensibly for coffee and cakes, but the real reason was so she could show off the koi carp she and her husband Harold had recently introduced to their pond to augment the goldfish and shebunkins.

As befitting her station in life, Mrs Wisbech's house, situated in the Mickleover area of Derby, was a large detached mock-Tudor dwelling. Although the house was impressive it was its walled garden, which had once been selected as 'Garden of the Week' in *Derbyshire Life*, that was Mrs Wisbech's pride and joy. A traditional English garden, with Japanese influences, everything in it was organic. Until today that is.

Both Mrs Bean and Miss Preece suspected that the invitation might have an ulterior motive as the only other occasion on which Mrs Wisbech had invited them round for coffee and cakes was the time she'd had the new barbecue built. Despite Mrs Wisbech's likely hidden agenda Mrs Bean, although she had better things to do, thought it prudent to attend. She had a speeding charge coming up shortly and there was every chance Mrs Wisbech would be sitting on the bench. For her part Miss Preece was aware that Mrs Wisbech was on the board of governors of her school. This had been more than enough to guarantee the teacher's attendance.

"Oh by the way, there's something you simply must see while you're here," said Mrs Wisbech, trying to sound as though the thought had just occurred to her. "It's out in the garden."

She got to her feet and made for the French windows, walking in the 'Here's my head my arse is coming' gait affected by overweight women of a certain age. Mrs Bean and Miss Preece exchanged resigned glances, put their cups on the coffee table and dutifully followed.

The French windows led into to the back garden. Mrs Wisbech was about to step outside when she remembered that koi carp are shown to their best advantage when feeding. "You go through, I'll be with you in a moment," she said, then made for the kitchen while Mrs Bean and Miss Preece continued into the garden.

"Oh my word!" said Mrs Bean, a moment later, obviously impressed on seeing the contents of the pond.

"Do you like them?" called Mrs Wisbech, pleased. "Such lovely colours aren't they."

"There's more than one?" said Mrs Bean. "I can see only the one."

"No, there are two. However one of them spends most of the time lurking behind the fishing gnome," explained Mrs Wisbech.

Mrs Bean didn't think much of the colours of the one she could see, predominately pink with a splash of red here and there and a yellow head, but was too polite to say so. She couldn't see the one that was apparently lurking behind the fishing gnome to see if its colours were more to her taste.

The night before, when the playful breeze that had caused Grimshaw so much trouble with the inflatable rubber woman had finally stopped being playful, it had deposited its cargo in the farmer's field some half a mile away, where it had almost interested a bull. Becoming playful again overnight the breeze had then lifted Glorious Gloria once more, borne her a further mile and deposited her in the pond in the back garden of Mrs Wisbech's house on Kennerley Road.

Now, returning with a box of floating fish hoops, Mrs Wisbech saw the inflatable rubber woman, stopped dead in her tracks, screamed and threw her hands and the box of fish food high in the air. A good handful of the fish hoops cascaded from the box and landed in the pool. A brightly-coloured koi carp suddenly appeared from underneath the inflatable rubber woman and started feeding voraciously on the fish hoops, causing the water to bubble and foam, as Mrs Wisbech had intended, but not exactly by the method by which she'd intended. The first koi was quickly joined by the koi from behind the fishing gnome.

"Who.....who put that thing there?" gasped Mrs Wisbech, absolutely outraged, pointing at Glorious Gloria.

"Didn't you?" said Mrs Bean.

"Me?" Mrs Wisbech looked at her with disbelief at the very idea.

"Isn't it what you wanted us to see?" asked Miss Preece.

"Well of course it isn't," said Mrs Wisbech, most affronted. "Why on earth would I put a disgusting thing like that in my pond?"

"Well I couldn't say, really" admitted Miss Preece. A thought came to her. "To frighten away herons, perhaps?"

"It may frighten herons but it doesn't seem to be causing the fish too much concern," observed Mrs Bean, as one of the koi, having made short work of the food in the pond, spotted a fish hoop that had landed on the inflatable rubber woman, leapt out of the water and plucked it expertly from her belly. "Oh I don't know though," she added, when on its journey back into the water the koi got itself temporarily stuck between Glorious Gloria's breasts, before frantically wriggling itself free and landing in the pond with a loud 'plop'.

"It must be some sort of sick joke," said Mrs Wisbech. "Probably revenge, retribution from someone I've had to fine heavily or send to pri.......oh my God!"

"What is it?" said Miss Preece, concerned, as most of the colour suddenly drained from Mrs Wisbech's face.

"The landscape gardener is due to arrive at any moment to repair the flags on my patio! I mustn't have him seeing that thing. Good Lord it will be all over the neighbourhood. We must get it out of there at once. At once."

Mrs Bean noted that the pond was very large and that the inflatable rubber woman was in the middle of it, well out of reach. She made this point.

"Perhaps you could wade in and get it, Mrs Wisbech?" suggested Miss Preece, helpfully. "Is it very deep?"

"Four feet. We had to have it deepened especially for the koi, they have to be in deep water."

Mrs Bean just resisted the temptation to tell Mrs Wisbech that she would be in deep water herself if the landscape gardener turned up while Glorious Gloria was still bathing in the pond. Instead she offered a solution to the problem.

"Throw stones."

"What?"

"We should throw stones."

Mrs Wisbech rolled her eyes. "I realise that throwing stones at it might dissipate my anger somewhat, Mrs Bean, but how on earth is it going to get the blessed thing out of my pond?"

Mrs Bean explained. "Not at it, near to it. So that the water creates waves and moves it nearer to us; then we'll be able to grab hold of it and pull it out. I remember one off my Brownies doing it when her ball landed in the canal."

"Ah. Yes, excellent idea, Mrs Bean." Mrs Wisbech looked around for stones. "Perhaps a few pebbles from the pathway might do the trick?"

The three ladies each armed themselves with a handful of pebbles and commenced to throw them into the pond as near to the inflatable rubber woman as their stone throwing skills allowed. If just one of them had thrown pebbles the idea might have worked. However Mrs Bean's pebbles, which landed on the far side of Glorious Gloria, were cancelled out by Miss Preece's, which landed on the near side of her. Most of Mrs Wisbech's pebbles landed on her. Consequently all that happened was that Glorious Gloria began to bob up and down like some sort of erotic buoy.

"This isn't going to work," frowned Mrs Wisbech.

Mrs Bean thought she'd heard something and cupped a hand to her ear. "Was that the front doorbell? Your landscape gardener perhaps?" she said, half hoping it was.

"Ignore it," said Mrs Wisbech.

"Larger pebbles," said Miss Preece. "We need larger pebbles. These pebbles aren't causing large enough waves to move it to any degree. Do you have any larger pebbles, Mrs Wisbech?"

Mrs Wisbech thought for a moment. "Bricks!" she said, suddenly inspired. "There were some bricks over from when we had the barbecue built. I think Harold put them in the greenhouse."

Six red bricks were obtained from the greenhouse.

"Leave it to me," said Mrs Bean, rolling up her sleeves. "I always won the throwing the rounders ball competition in the school sports."

The first brick, launched by Mrs Bean with all her skill at throwing the rounders ball, scored a direct hit on the inflatable rubber woman, bounced off it at right angles and decapitated the fishing gnome.

"Sorry," said Mrs Bean.

"Damn!"

"Frightfully sorry, Mrs Wisbech."

"I suppose Harold might be able to repair it," said Mrs Wisbech, but without much hope.

Whether Harold's gnome repairing skills would be adequate was unclear. What was very clear was that he wouldn't be able to do much about the koi carp on which Mrs Bean's next brick scored a direct hit, killing it instantaneously.

What remained of the colour in Mrs Wisbech's face drained instantly. She flung her hands in the air. "My God! Harold will go mad. They cost us five hundred pounds each, we've only had them for a week."

"Look," said Miss Preece, pointing at Glorious Gloria. The resultant turbulence from the two bricks had caused her to turn over onto her face. "It's turned turtle."

"I wish it would turn *into* a blasted turtle," said Mrs Wisbech. "And paddle off somewhere far away." She turned on Mrs Bean and shook a warning finger. "Now you aren't to throw any more bricks, do you hear. I don't want you killing the other one."

"At least now that it's turned over you can't see its enormous breasts," consoled Miss Preece.

"You can see its enormous bottom," said Mrs Wisbech, not even slightly consoled. "And that horrible thong thing between its legs. Which is a more horrific sight than its bosom, if anything." She looked at the others desperately. "We just have to get it out of there somehow, ladies."

Mrs Bean cocked an ear. "Is that the doorbell again?"

"Bugger the doorbell!" said Mrs Wisbech. She bit her lip. "Sorry, forgive my language, I don't....it's all this...." She spread her hands in a gesture of hopelessness.

"Perhaps we could pop it?" suggested Miss Preece. "It would sink to the bottom and out of sight if we could manage to pop it. Have you anything with which we could pop it, Mrs Wisbech?"

Mrs Wisbech thought for a moment. "Well there's the carving knife, that might do the trick I suppose," she said, but with no great conviction. "Or a screwdriver, perhaps." Then, suddenly inspired: "Harold's bow and arrow! He's a member of the Derbyshire Bowmen, he's got a bow and arrow." She made for the door. "If the landscape gardener tries to get in through the back gate keep him at bay."

Two minutes later she returned with a large crossbow. "Here it is. This will do the trick."

"Is that a bow and arrow?" queried Miss Preece, looking at it uncertainly.

"That's how they are nowadays," said Mrs Bean. "All knobs and sights and fiddly things. I saw them in the Commonwealth Games, terribly complicated; if Robin Hood came back and tried to fire one he wouldn't have a clue."

"I'm afraid I share Robin Hood's ignorance of them," said Mrs Wisbech, looking at the bow and scratching her head.

"I think I should be able to manage to fire it, if I may?" offered Mrs Bean.

Mrs Wisbech wasn't sure. "You didn't win the bow and arrow competition at your school sports by any chance?"

"No. But you might recall that one of the two bricks that I threw hit its target?" said Mrs Bean, a bit miffed.

"I recall that the other one hit one of the koi carp we paid five hundred pounds for and that I only have one five hundred pounds koi carp remaining." said Mrs Wisbech, with feeling. She thought about it for a moment, then shrugged her shoulders. "However, as I don't know how to fire the blessed thing...." She handed the bow to Mrs Bean. "But please, please be careful."

Mrs Bean loaded the bow as Mrs Wisbech and Miss Preece looked on, the former still by no means happy about it. Miss Preece wrinkled her brow. "Is that the arrow?"

"The bolt, you call it," said Mrs Bean, knowledgably.

Mrs Wisbech started to feel a little better about it. If Mrs Bean knew that the business part of the weapon was no longer called an arrow, but a bolt, she obviously knew what she was talking about. But words were cheap. Could she fire the thing? And even if she could fire it, could she hit the target, could she hit the horrible inflatable rubber woman that was scandalising her pond with its filthy presence?

She could. Gloriously. The wonderful, quite wonderful Mrs Bean released the bolt from the bow and almost immediately Glorious Gloria exploded with a loud bang as it scored a direct hit. Then continued on and hit the other koi carp, which surfaced two seconds later, stone dead and draped in part of Glorious Gloria's bottom.

"Sorry. Sorry about that, Mrs Wisbech" said Mrs Bean, full of remorse. She brightened slightly. "However I did pop the inflatable rubber woman."

"Yes, you wouldn't recognise it now," added Miss Preece. "What's left of it."

Mrs Wisbech sighed. "I suppose that's something to be grateful for."

Miss Preece noticed that a small card had been washed to the pond's edge. "What's that?" she said, pointing it out.

Mrs Wisbech bent to pick it out of the water. There was

some writing on it. She read it out. "*Glorious Gloria. With the compliments of An Hour In Bed. Enjoy.*"

CHAPTER SEVENTEEN

Pugh's secretary popped her head round the door. "The Junior Ministers are here, Mr Pugh."

Pugh buried his head in his hands and groaned. "Tell them to go away."

"I'll send them in shall I?"

Pugh nodded glumly; he'd have to see them sooner or later. He would far rather have spent his time trying to come up with a way of making An Hour In Bed a viable concern again than listening to Dowell, Hilversum and Brick, for surely there must be at least one way. However a month ago The Prime Minister had charged his Cabinet Ministers with producing new vote-winning ideas that might be incorporated into an election-winning manifesto. Ideas from the Department of Transport had to be in by tomorrow's deadline and as Pugh hadn't come up with anything he hoped his trio of underlings might have come up with something.

Pugh's three whipping boys trooped in. He barely acknowledged them with a grunt.

As he waited for them to seat themselves he searched their faces to see if any signs of having had a good idea had left themselves etched there. He fully anticipated seeing nothing but blank canvasses but both Dowell and Hilversum looked even more pleased with themselves than usual, so maybe they'd managed to break the habits of a lifetime and come up with something sensible.

Pugh wasted no time on pleasantries or small talk. "Well, what have you got for me?" he said, before they'd hardly settled. The Junior Ministers each waited for one of the others to speak first. Pugh made their minds up for them and picked out the Parliamentary Under Secretary in charge of Aviation. "Justin?"

"Well I was thinking we might do something to reduce the time people have to spend getting through all the airport security checks we've had to impose since 9/11."

"And?"

"Well clearly people are getting really pissed off with it, so it's something they'd really appreciate. I mean they're spending half their holiday queuing. Happened to me when I flew to Rome the other week. Three bloody hours it took me. Anyway it's high time we pulled the plug on it. Just limit the search to people who look like they might be terrorists."

"People who look like they might be terrorists?"

"Middle Eastern types, Iraquis, Iranians, Afghans, swarthy looking people with dark complexions and moustaches."

"What about women?"

Dowell sniggered. "Well that description covers most of the Middle Eastern women I've ever come across. But we could specify all people who wear the hijab or burka. I think it would be a real vote catcher. Quite clearly it would be very popular with the electorate."

Jim Brick intervened. "It wouldn't be very popular with people with black moustaches who happened to be a bit dark-skinned. Quite a few MPs are like that."

Pugh turned to Brick. "You don't like the idea then, Jim?" Although he disliked Brick immensely Pugh knew that he often talked a lot of sense, even if it was sense he didn't necessarily agree with.

"Oh I'm not saying that," said Brick. "No, I'm just saying it might be a bit awkward; a bit difficult to implement. No, I think it's an excellent idea. I'm sure if we put it to Phil he'd be bound to go for it."

Warning bells immediately rang in Pugh's head. There was nothing Brick would like better than for him to go to Phil with some crackpot idea and come back with egg on his face. If Brick said something was a good idea you could bet your boots it was a bad idea and could only result in amounts of egg in large proportions descending on his physiognomy. He nodded sagely and said: "Yes, well I think we'd best put that one on the back burner for the time being, Justin." He turned his attention to Hilversum. "Anything we can do on roads and rail, Tony? That might encourage people to vote for us?"

"Yes, I think we should shut down the railways."

Pugh raised an eyebrow. "Shut them down?"

"Think about it. Clearly everyone would then have to travel by road. Clearly people who haven't got a car would have to buy one or failing that walk wherever they wanted to get to. Clearly if they chose to buy a car it would mean more jobs for the motor industry. And most clearly of all, if they chose to walk they'd all be fitter and less of a drain on the Health Service and we'd save millions."

Although Pugh could see workers in the car industry being overjoyed and falling over themselves to vote Labour should Hilversum's idea be implemented he immediately saw a snag. "I thought the roads were overcrowded already?"

"We'll build more roads. Clearly this would create thousands and thousands of jobs in the construction industry. Jobs that could be filled by all the people who were made redundant when we closed down the railways - after they had received suitable training of course - which would bring thousands of jobs to the job training industry."

"And these roads? Given that there isn't any room for any more roads without making compulsory purchase orders, which would cost the country billions in compensation, where would they be built?"

Hilversum smiled. "On the railways. Tear up the old railway lines and build roads on them. Which would clearly have the effect of re-vitalising and creating thousands of jobs in the scrap metal and steel-recycling industries. Or alternatively we could leave the rails as they are and fit all new cars with an extra set of wheels, which they could then use on the railways when they drove directly onto them after leaving the roads."

Pugh looked sharply at Hilversum. Was he taking the piss? Or could he actually be serious? One could never be sure with Oxbridge upstarts. He'd been serious when he'd suggested making the M25 a one-way system, alternate days clockwise and anti-clockwise, and the Prime Minister had almost gone for that. Help was at hand in his dilemma, however, as from the corner of his eye he noticed Brick shake his head and grimace. "I can see you're not too keen on the idea, Jim?" he said, turning to Brick.

"You can say that again."

For his part Pugh thought Hilversum's plan to be one of the most stupid ideas he'd ever heard in his life, and as a Cabinet Minister of four years standing he'd heard more than a few; however if Brick intimated it was a bad idea that meant it was a good idea. "Well I think it's an excellent idea," he said. He smirked at Brick to show him he had his number, before continuing. "Well done, Tony. I'll put it to Phil." He turned his attention back to Brick. "And you, Jim, have you managed to come up with anything?"

Brick shook his head. "Not in my department, no. The only thing I thought we might give a try is in Justin's area."

"And is?"

"Well I thought we might do something about single car occupancy. Penalise the sole occupants of cars. Help out the situation with our crowded roads. I believe the idea was mooted a year or two ago but that was as far as it went, never got beyond the White Paper stage. Remember, Justin?"

Dowell shook his head. "Must have been before my time."

"It was designed to encourage car sharing, to get drivers to actively seek out people making the same journey. Which would mean of course they were no longer the sole occupant of their car and thus not liable to pay the single occupancy penalty."

Hilversum didn't like the sound of it at all. "This would apply to Members of Parliament too, one would assume?"

"We have chauffeurs, don't we," said Brick, patiently. "We never drive ourselves; the single occupancy charge would never apply to us."

"I do," said Pugh, recalling his visit to Ramsbottom to view his inheritance, and the many other times he had dispensed with the services of his chauffeur for one reason or another. "I drove myself about four hundred miles only the other day. And I certainly don't want to be paying a levy for driving myself. I...." He was about to go on to say that he quite enjoyed emitting some carbon by bombing down the motorway whenever he felt the need of it, when he suddenly stopped.

Dowell didn't think much of the idea either. "Besides, I thought we were supposed to be coming up with vote-catching ideas?" he scoffed. "I can't see a single car occupancy tax getting us many votes from car drivers."

"You have to look at the bigger picture, Justin. And the bigger picture tells us...."

Pugh, now with a strange light in his eyes, suddenly burst

in. "Yes well thank you all for your time gentlemen, that will be all." He got to his feet and indicated to the others to do likewise. "Time waits for no man."

"Don't you want to know the bigger picture?"

But Pugh didn't. He had his own bigger picture now. And it was a wonderful, beautiful picture, a blockbuster of a picture in wide screen 3D with Dolby stereophonic sound, or whatever sound wonderful blockbusters came with nowadays. It had come to him in a flash. A eureka moment. It was his good idea.

After ushering, almost pushing the Junior Ministers out of his office, Pugh took a moment to compose himself, then sat down and wrote out his good idea on a piece of paper so that he couldn't possibly forget it. Well he couldn't forget it, he knew that, for it was such a wonderfully good idea, such an unforgettable good idea, but he needed to have graphic, physical evidence of it, just to prove it.

It looked even better on paper. He wrote it out again underneath. It looked twice as good. He put it in the top drawer of his desk for safe keeping. Five seconds later he opened the drawer and looked inside. It was still there. He took it out and looked at it again. He pinched himself. Yes, he wasn't dreaming. He folded it up, kissed it, put it back and locked the drawer so it couldn't get out and no one could get at it.

For the next twenty four hours he didn't do anything about his good idea. He had never in his life had an idea even half as good, and he might never have another one, so he wanted to drink it in for a while, bathe in it, luxuriate in it, wallow in it. For this was no ordinary good idea, this wasn't his mobile massage parlour good idea, this was an idea on a much higher level, the very highest level, it was as good an idea as good ideas could come; a gold-plated copper-bottomed all-singing all-dancing good idea.

The first thing he did on entering his office the following day was unlock his drawer and take out the piece of paper on which he had written his good idea. He looked at it; the words were still there, all in the same order just the same as when he'd written them, they hadn't mysteriously and heartbreakingly shuffled themselves around and formed themselves into a bad idea.

It was a nice day so he put the piece of paper in his pocket and took his idea for a walk round the block. The streets were busy with people going here and there about their daily business. Pugh smiled to himself. They didn't know that in his pocket he had the best idea since sliced bread. On the corner of Page Street and Regency Street, suddenly realising the possible threat that people in the street might present, he took the idea out of his pocket, took his shoe off, put it in his shoe and put it back on; it would be safer there, you never knew, someone could quite easily pick his pocket, and his idea along with it, and there was a chance, even if it was a billion to one chance, that he might have some sort of brainstorm or be struck with amnesia and forget all about his good idea.

Back in his office he told Myra that he wasn't accepting any phone calls that morning and started making plans to put his good idea into practice, to make it work, to get it to turn him into a multi-millionaire, which surely such a good idea would do. He realised that the stumbling block, the fly in the ointment, would be Prime Minister Phil Good, for without his co-operation his good idea would be for nothing. However stumbling blocks could be cleared out of the way, and flies could be removed from ointment, rendering it useable again, it was just a matter of finding a way to remove them.

The problem was that he needed a favour of Phil and Phil just wasn't the sort of man who did favours. He was a man who accepted favours. To get him on his side Pugh knew he would have to appeal to the Prime Minister's baser instincts. And as no one's instincts were baser than Phil Good's such an approach would be bound to cost him a pretty penny.

A lesson Pugh had absorbed early in his career was that you could get your own way with most people if you gave them enough bullshit. However around the same time he had also learned that you can't bullshit a bullshitter, and as Phil was a bullshitter *par excellence* that route to success was not open to him on this occasion.

Fortunately he had also come to appreciate that fifty per cent of something is better than a hundred per cent of nothing, and had adopted this maxim as a guiding principle in life. He now applied it again, bit the bullet and asked Myra to get him the Prime Minister on the line.

CHAPTER EIGHTEEN

Rap...rap...rap. Once again Willoughby rapped the dildo on the table top to bring the monthly meeting of Vigilantes Against Sex Toys to order. Once again Miss Preece visibly blanched. Willoughby smiled at her and the rest of the usual suspects, their ranks swelled this evening by a new face. "Good evening, ladies and gentlemen," he said. "Before we start tonight's meeting it is my great pleasure to announce that we have added a new convert to our ranks." He turned his smile on the new member. "Allow me to introduce Elton Arbuckle."

All the members turned to look at Arbuckle, who shuffled his feet self-consciously as he returned their smiles of welcome.

"Welcome to our little organisation," said Mrs Bean. "I am Mrs Bean, Flora Bean. Elton or Mr Arbuckle, which do you prefer?"

Arbuckle would have preferred to be incognito, and preferably somewhere else. He was already beginning to think that maybe it hadn't been such good idea to join VAST, after all. Not if it was going to be anything like what he'd witnessed in the few minutes since he'd joined. There had already almost been a fight, when a man who looked like a Taliban rebel had told another man he was glad he'd lost his job if it meant he wouldn't be leaving sex toys on the council tip where his children could get stuck in them. The chairman banging a huge artificial penis on the table to bring the meeting to order didn't augur well either.

Arbuckle had learned about the activities of VAST quite

by accident. In the course of his studies he was in the habit of typing the words 'Inflatable Rubber Women' into one or other of the internet search engines from time to time, just to see what came up. Usually it was just the websites of sellers of sex toys, and he'd already explored all those, but if you got beyond the first pages of Google and Ask things began to improve. Websites other than ones solely employed in supplying the nation's perverted tastes were listed. One night he had chanced upon the website of VAST. Included in the search engine's brief details were the words '...*we must not rest in our labours until every last inflatable rubber woman has been removed from the face of the earth....*'

He had logged on to VAST's small website, www.vast.com, and had discovered that the words had been taken from a speech given by Willoughby at one of the group's meetings.

After quickly browsing through the website Arbuckle had reached the conclusion that VAST seemed to be a fairly innocuous organisation, a bit weird perhaps, but relatively harmless. However as a student of inflatable rubber women he naturally wanted to know everything there was to know about them. Up until then he had only ever met people who were for them, he hadn't been aware there were any people against them, although when he thought about it he realised that it was more than a probability. For example he couldn't imagine that sex dolls would be exactly flavour of the month with the wives of the men who owned them.

But some of the members of VAST would be men, he supposed. What had men got against sex dolls? He decided it might not be a bad thing to join VAST in order to find out. It might broaden the scope of his thesis, take it into another area, allow him to go off at a tangent maybe; the more he packed into his dissertation the better his chances would be of obtaining a first class degree with hons, and along with it some first class sex, with or without hons, the fruits that surely such a degree would bring with it.

"Mr Arbuckle is a student," said Willoughby. "Mathematics I believe you said, Mr Arbuckle?"

"Pure and Applied," lied Arbuckle, secure in the knowledge that if there were any maths wizards amongst them who started asking awkward questions he would be more than able to cope, having an 'A' level in each of the disciplines.

"Excellent, smiled Willoughby. He addressed the meeting. "Now before we start the meeting proper I would like you all to listen to this." He produced a pocket tape recorder, placed it on the desk and switched it on. Seconds later it began to play.

"Will you, Anne Marie, take this man to be thy lawful wedded wife?"

"I will."

"That was you."

"It wasn't, it was Anne Marie."

"It was you, Mr Perkins. I was watching you. You said 'I will' out of the corner of your mouth."

"No, I was sucking my tooth. And while you were watching me sucking my tooth my bride....my future bride....said 'I Will'. "

"It is not a bride, Mr Perkins, it is an inflatable rubber woman."

"What? No you've got it all wrong Vicar, it's my bride-to-be Anne Marie."

"It is an inflatable rubber woman, Mr Perkins. If you were let go of its hand it would float away."

"Now let's not be silly."

"It already has floated away once. It took us twenty minutes to get it down from the belfry."

"Please continue with the wedding ceremony, Vicar, you're keeping all the guests waiting."

"I am not marrying you to an inflatable rubber woman, Mr Perkins. And that is my final word on the matter!"

"Anne Marie is not an inflatable rubber woman. An inflatable rubber woman in a wedding dress? Don't make me laugh."

"She's not wearing a wedding dress, she's wearing a bra and G-string."

"Now she is. She lost her wedding dress when she floated up to the belfry and got it caught on the bells...."

Willoughby switched off the tape. "Yes well I think we've all heard enough of that rubbish."

"What was it?" queried Mrs Wisbech.

"An extract from a so-called radio comedy series." He snorted. "That's right, they're making jokes about sex toys on the radio now. Lord Reith would turn in his grave."

"Absolutely disgraceful."

"My sentiments entirely, Mrs Wisbech. I came across it quite by accident. The Willoughby radio is usually permanently set on Radio Four, with the odd excursion into Classic FM, but Mildred must have been listening to something or other on one of the other channels. When I switched on at my usual time what you have just been listening to came on. You can imagine my horror, I was expecting *Gardener's Question Time*."

"Oh you poor thing," sympathised Mrs Bean.

Willoughby looked around. "I can see from your faces that it sits as uneasily with the rest of you as it did with me."

A few of the members made noises of agreement.

Whether it sat uneasily with Flannery or not, the priest

didn't indicate. However Flannery himself was sitting very uneasily as, unable to readily come by a spiked suit as worn by the priest in *The Da Vinci Code*, he had stuffed his vest and underpants with crushed walnut shells. A piece of sharp shell that had lodged in his bum cleavage was now threatening to enter his anus, causing him to squirm in discomfort.

Willoughby noticed this. "I notice that you are particularly uncomfortable, Father Flannery."

"Oh indeed," said Flannery, wishing he'd gone along with his original inclination to leave the walnut shells whole.

"I hope the trauma of hearing that tripe on the radio didn't leave you too upset, Mr Willoughby?" said Seal, concerned.

"I shall write to the Director General of the BBC about it, copy to the Head of Radio," said Mrs Wisbech.

"Write?" Cleaver spat out, suddenly taking a keener interest in the proceedings. "Write? What good is that going to do? We're always writing to people; and what happens? I'll tell you what happens. Nothing. Sod all."

"I'm afraid Mr Cleaver is right," said Grimshaw, nodding his agreement. He turned to Mrs Wisbech. "Which reminds me, what happened about that barber's pole business?"

"I wrote to them again."

"And?"

Mrs Wisbech, obviously embarrassed, looked at Willoughby. The chairman came to her support. "They said they were considering adding a pair of bollocks to it; if you'll pardon my French."

Grimshaw shrugged. "Need I say more?"

"What we want is action," said Cleaver. "We won't get anywhere until we start taking action."

"And what precise action are you suggesting we should

take?" said Willoughby, guardedly.

Cleaver didn't need a second invitation. "Militant action. Physical action. Up and at 'em in their perverted faces action."

While being all for a more positive approach Seal felt that a degree of caution should be exercised. "The policeman in me is telling me that we shouldn't rush into something we might later regret," he warned.

"Thank you, Mr Seal."

Cleaver was unabashed. "I mean take this inflatable rubber women business. What we should be doing is targeting a firm that makes them. Making an example of them."

"And how might we do that?"

"We could chain ourselves to their railings," offered Mrs Bean, dramatically.

"Chain ourselves to their railings?" Cleaver scoffed. "What good would that do?"

Mrs Wisbech defended her sister-in-arms. "It got women the vote, I seem to recall."

"It would certainly make them sit up and take notice," added Miss Preece.

"Perhaps just the ladies could chain themselves to the railings?" suggested Willoughby, warming a little to the idea of a more militant stance. "But as far as the men are concerned.....?" In the hope of getting practical suggestions he left the rest of the sentence hanging in the air.

Cleaver eagerly grabbed hold of it. "Sabotage. Sabotage their factory, that's what we need to do. Wreck their machines. Put them out of action for a month or two. Stop them manufacturing the fucking things."

"Language, please, Mr Cleaver," said Mrs Wisbech.

"Technically he's right though," offered Mrs Bean. "They

are fu....what Mr Cleaver said they were."

"And he's right about what we should do about it," added Grimshaw, a man with just as much cause to hate inflatable rubber women as Cleaver.

"And in what way do you suggest we sabotage them?" said Willoughby.

Cleaver was in no doubt. "Set fire to their factory. Burn the place. Raze it to the ground. Gut the bloody place."

Mrs Wisbech stepped in. "Need I remind you that you have just spent a month at Her Majesty's pleasure for setting fire to things, Mr Cleaver."

"Yes, I really don't think we should consider fire as an option," said Willoughby. "In fact we won't be doing."

Khan suddenly leapt to his feet, his eyes gleaming with blood lust. "Go for their joculars!" He raised his hook high in the air. "Wouldn't make disgusting rubber women if they got this though their joculars," he continued, bringing his arm down in a flashing arc of metal.

While Willoughby appreciated this approach could well be very effective he doubted the practicality of it. "No doubt, Mr Khan, but we can't go about piercing people's jugular veins just because they're manufacturing something we don't like."

"No, but we can pierce the things we don't like that they are manufacturing," said Miss Preece. "We can pierce holes in the inflatable rubber women so that the perverts who buy them can't blow them up."

"Yes, that would slow them down a bit," agreed Willoughby. He warmed to the idea. "Yes, that would seem to be a capital suggestion, Miss Preece." He looked around the meeting. There were no signs of dissent, so he continued. "All those in favour say 'Aye'." He looked at them in turn, inviting their votes.

"Aye," said Mr Grimshaw.

"Aye," said Mr Seal.

"Aye," said Fr Flannery.

"Aye," said Mr Cleaver.

"Aye," said Mrs Wisbech.

"Aye," said Mrs Bean.

"Aye," said Miss Preece.

"Aye," said Mr Khan.

"Fuck me", said Arbuckle, though fortunately only to himself. "Just who the hell are these weirdos?"

"I can see you haven't quite made your mind up, Mr Arbuckle," said Willoughby, on failing to elicit an 'Aye' from him. He brushed it off. "We can understand, I assure you, your being new to all this. We won't be at all offended if you choose not to join us when we mount our operation."

"No." Arbuckle quickly assured him. "Of course I'll come." If he were to stop these mad people carrying out their plan the last thing he wanted was to be left out. "Please, count me in."

Willoughby smiled. "That's settled then." He put on a sterner expression before continuing, to the group in general. "However I feel that the sort of action we have decided upon is only suitable for the men to undertake. One never knows, we may clash with security guards or the like. There could quite possibly be violence."

"I agree wholeheartedly," said Mrs Wisbech. "However it is my wish to take an active part in the strike. And I'm sure I speak for the other ladies." She looked at Mrs Bean and Miss Preece, who both eagerly nodded their agreement. "Very well then, I vote that the three ladies chain themselves to their railings."

Willoughby concurred. "Excellent. Such a dramatic action

is bound to bring them adverse publicity. All that remains is for us to select a target. So which manufacturer of inflatable rubber women shall we attack?"

"An Hour In Bed", said Cleaver, Grimshaw, Flannery, Seal, Mrs Wisbech, Mrs Bean and Miss Preece at once, in unison, and with great feeling.

"An Whore In Bed," said Khan. Not having had the same recent and unfortunate contact with the products of An Hour In Bed as the others the Afghan wouldn't have known the firm from Adam, or maybe Allah, but there was no way he was going to be left out.

Willoughby felt Khan's slight error with the name of the company to be quite apposite and hardly worth correcting. He smiled. "That appears to be settled then."

The meeting then went into detail about how the strike on the An Hour In Bed factory might be realised. Arbuckle, taken completely by surprise at the turn of events, and still more than a little in awe of these mad men and women that fate had brought him into contact with, sat quietly and took in every detail. He could scarcely comprehend it. These people, these morons – one of them was an ex-copper, one a Justice of the Peace and another a vicar for God's sake - were actually going to mount an attack on An Hour in Bed; on his benefactors, on the firm who only days ago had generously taken him under its wing with the gift of a month's work experience.

In the eight days he'd owned Bouncy Beyoncé, during which time he'd had sex with her at least once every day, Arbuckle had come to fully appreciate the benefit of having enjoyable sex on tap. He wanted as many men as possible to have the same benefit. Which they wouldn't be having if the country's largest supplier of inflatable rubber women was sabotaged by a bunch of lunatics.

He couldn't let them get away with it of course. He wouldn't. But how to stop them?

CHAPTER NINETEEN

On the wall behind the 10 Downing Street desk of Phil Good MP, Prime Minister and First Lord of the Treasury, was a large banner which bore a photograph of the smiling Good along with the slogan 'Get the Phil Good Factor.' The words were a clever if rather obvious play on the expression 'feel good factor', the slogan dreamt up by the advertising firm of Clough and Bonham (known throughout the profession as Bluff and Con 'em), that had swept the Labour Leader to power at the last general election with a majority of a hundred and ten. The fact that Phil Good had never in his entire political career done a single thing which might cause people to feel good had been completely lost on the electorate. However the fact that he'd done nothing to make them feel good since he'd been elected Prime Minister had not been lost on them, and was why he stood about as much chance of being voted back into Number 10 in the forthcoming election as Osama bin Laden.

On the opposite wall were another seventeen photographs. Each of them was of the Prime Minister glad-handing visiting foreign Heads of State. Good jokingly referred to the photographs as 'The Rogues Gallery'. On seeing them many other people did likewise, but they weren't joking, especially with regard to Phil Good.

Taking pride of place on the walls was a cartoon of the Prime Minister, a present from the political cartoonist Dirk, from whom Good had requested the original after seeing it in a newspaper. It depicted a caricature of the smiling Prime Minister with what purported to be the Good coat of arms, along with the family motto '*Trickier than a barrelful of monkeys*', which the cartoonist had meant as a slight on Good's character but which Good had taken as a compliment.

Aged just forty six, young for a Prime Minister by British standards, Good was a handsome man, his good looks tarnished only by the smarminess that manifests itself in the features of most politicians.

In much the same way that Hugh Pugh found a safe haven behind his Junior Ministers, Phil Good took refuge behind his Cabinet Ministers. As most of his Cabinet Ministers adopted Pugh's principal of hiding behind his Junior Ministers it had the effect of erecting yet another barrier between The Prime Minister and those who sought to take him to task over his many shortcomings. He was as an Army Chief of Staff in time of war, directing operations from the safety of HQ whilst his infantry took the bullets at the Front.

A political commentator had once suggested that Good should have a plaque on his desk which read '*The buck never gets here*'. Instead he had a photograph of his family. Like former Labour Prime Minister Tony Blair, Good had a wife, Fleur, who was also a lawyer, and with whom he'd had four children. However the similarity to Blair ended there as Good's children were all girls and his wife was halfway presentable.

On leaving Oxford, with a First in Law and a 2.1 in Political Science, Good had gone directly into politics as a researcher at Labour Party Headquarters. The only thing he had researched was how to get ahead in politics without having to do very much. His researches had informed him that by far the best way to achieve this was by becoming a spin doctor. So for the next two years he had worshipped at the temple of Blair's Director of Communications and

Strategy, Alastair Campbell. After twelve months of finding out exactly how Campbell went about the business of saying one thing whilst meaning another, then putting it into practice, the only person who didn't dislike him was his mother. After a further six months of soaking up Campbell's poison even his mother didn't like him. And after the final six months he had become such an absolute twat that he had no difficulty spinning himself into a job as Personal Adviser and Chief of Staff to the Chancellor of the Exchequer.

Being privy to all the financial changes the Chancellor of the Exchequer necessarily has to implement in the course of ruining the country's finances had made Good a millionaire by the time he was thirty, at which point he became a Member of Parliament in the safe seat of Bletchwich North. Eight years and two Parliaments on saw him as Shadow Chancellor of the Exchequer. Two years later he was elected Leader.

When Pugh had requested a meeting with him Good had groaned inwardly, his usual reaction when the Transport Minister wanted to see him. It was bad enough seeing him at Cabinet meetings. Pugh would be on the make, he knew; he had requested the meeting to report back personally on vote-winning ideas, but there would be a hidden agenda, there always was with Pugh. He would probably be bringing up the peerage thing again, despite his being kicked back the other three times he'd asked to be elevated to the Upper House. (The second time he'd brought it up Good had toyed with the idea of acceding to his request on the condition that he be known as Lord Lout of Loudmouth, but had decided that even that wasn't compensation enough for the dire prospect of Pugh swanning around Westminster dressed in ermine.)

In the event it turned out to be something even more

impossible than a peerage that Pugh was seeking. Good was already in a bad mood, having just spent over an hour on the phone in an effort to patch up Britain's special relationship with the United States. The Deputy Prime Minister, Dick Balding, had been quoted in the newspapers as saying that US President Richard Sole was not only an R Sole in name but an R Sole in nature and it hadn't gone down very well with the President. Good's mood hadn't been improved on hearing Pugh's opening gambit.

"Are you quite mad?" said Good, in reply to it. "Introduce a levy on single car occupancy? Fuck me, Hugh, I asked you to come up with vote-catching ideas and you come here with an idea that's going to lose us the vote of every car driver in the country!"

Pugh remained calm. He had expected such a reaction. "I think we can safely say we'll lose the next election, Phil."

"We will if we implement stupid fucking ideas like that!"

"We'll lose anyway."

"So? That doesn't mean we have to give it away!"

Pugh was aware that the hand of cards he had been dealt was not one that could be played close to the chest. It was the sort that had to be laid on the table, face up, out in the open, so it could be seen for what it was. He laid it out. "Losing the election will mean that people like you and me will have to look to the future, money-wise, Phil. Money-wise," he repeated, emphasising the word 'money'.

There was no need for the emphasis. Good's ears had pricked at the mention of his favourite word, as Pugh knew it would. "Money wise? What do you mean, money-wise?"

"Simply that you and me are in a position to make a lot of money, Phil. Serious money. If we go about it the right way."

The Prime Minister doubted very much if Pugh had the

brains to pick his nose, let alone come up with something likely to make a lot of money. However he was the last man in the world to dismiss a potential money-making opportunity out of hand. He sat back in his chair, formed his hands into a church steeple, then cocked his head to one side in the way that Fleur had told him he looked at his most impressive. "Go on, I'm listening."

"As I've already said, we implement a levy on single car occupancy. A big one. Very big, punitive, a grand a day, of that order; something big enough to make everybody but merchant bankers and footballers think twice before driving their car unless there's somebody sat in it with them." He paused for a moment before going on. "And once we've done that, what's going to happen?"

"Tell me."

"Some car drivers who don't want to pay the levy, or can't afford to pay it, are going to set up car-sharing schemes with people travelling to the same places. But a lot of them aren't going to bother. A lot of them are going to get round the problem by putting an artificial passenger in the seat alongside them, to fool the police into thinking they've got somebody travelling with them."

"An artificial passenger?"

"Something that looks like a passenger."

Good thought about it for a moment. "You reckon?"

"I reckon."

So did Good. He knew very little about the ordinary man in the street, or cared to, but one thing he did know was that he would try anything to avoid paying a penny more in taxes than absolutely necessary.

"They'll be using all sorts," Pugh went on. "Tailor's dummies; models from department store windows, what do they call them, mannequins; figures they've made themselves, like they make Guy Fawkes; cardboard cut-outs." He paused for effect. "And inflatable rubber women."

Good nodded. "Yes. Well why wouldn't they."

The only card in his hand that Pugh hadn't yet played was the joker. He played it now. "And I own the biggest inflatable rubber woman factory in the country. For artificial passenger, read inflatable rubber woman." Before continuing he took a moment to fondly recall travelling all the way from Ramsbottom to London with Willing Wilma in the passenger seat beside him, without so much as a single person batting an eyelid. "I've got one million of them at fifty quid a throw stock-piled and ready to go at the drop of a bit of legislation. I'm proposing to cut you in for twenty per cent of the profits." He sat back with a smug smile, confident that Good would go along with the idea.

"Forty."

Pugh winced, but only for the sake of appearances. He had been expecting Good to demand thirty per cent, in which case he would have settled for twenty-five. Now he himself would have to offer thirty and the Prime Minister would go to thirty five, which he'd have to accept. No matter, after his accountant had done a bit of creative accounting Good wouldn't even be getting twenty five, he'd be getting twenty if he was lucky. Good of course was well aware of this, but no matter, the ritual had to be acted out, the game had to be played, both men had to be seen to be unwilling to give up too much ground.

"Thirty, said Pugh."

"Thirty five."

"Done."

"Done," smiled Good, offering his hand.

Pugh now exercised a word of caution. He had a shrewd idea what the Prime Minister's reaction would be, but the point still had to be made nevertheless. "The Cabinet won't like it."

"The Cabinet," said Good, "can kiss my starboard bollock."

Pugh smiled to himself. He knew his man.

CHAPTER TWENTY

Two days later, when Pugh had revealed to Wainwright his plan to sell the million inflatable rubber women as artificial car passengers, the factory manager had immediately seen a snag. "But they're all contaminated, Mr Pugh," he said, scarcely able to credit Pugh's intentions.

Pugh and Wainwright were facing each other across the latter's desk. However it was Pugh who was seated in Wainwright's chair, having commandeered the manager's office on discovering it was An Hour In Bed's largest, and relegating the factory manager to a much smaller one next to the ladies toilets. "Where you'll be able to keep an eye on the women, they probably spend too much time gossiping in there anyway," Pugh had said.

Pugh couldn't see the reason for Wainwright's concern. "So?"

"Well you can't sell them if they're contaminated."

"Why not?"

"Well....I mean they're contaminated."

"So they're contaminated? People are going to use them as artificial passengers, not inflatable rubber women. The sales manager didn't raise any objections when I told him what we were doing. He said he looked forward to the new challenge."

"Yes well he would."

"What's that supposed to mean?"

"Well Mallory would sell horseshit as tobacco if he thought he could get away with it."

Pugh glared at him. "It sounds like he's sold you some horseshit if you ask me, because you've got horseshit to spare the amount of it you're giving me."

"Well I'm sorry, Mr Pugh, but I'm very uncomfortable with the idea. And for quite a few reasons."

There wasn't a single reason in the world that would make Pugh change his mind. He was interested to know what Wainwright's objections might be, nevertheless. "Such as?"

"Well for one, although we'll be selling the inflatable rubber women as artificial passengers they'll still really be inflatable rubber woman. And even though a man might have bought one to use as an artificial passenger, once he's realised it's an inflatable rubber woman he might....well, use it for the purpose for which it was originally intended."

"Well in that case he's got two for the price of one, hasn't he. Anyway that's beside...."

"But he might contaminate himself, Mr Pugh. Well he will contaminate himself, no doubt about it, if he...."

Pugh cut in impatiently. "Well that's his bloody lookout isn't it. He bought it to put it in the passenger seat of his car, not to fuck it whenever he got a bit randy; serve the bugger right if he does get contaminated."

"You wouldn't be saying that if you'd seen somebody who'd been contaminated, Mr Pugh, if you don't mind me saying so. They come out in this horrible...."

Pugh snapped. "I *am* somebody who's been contaminated. Thanks to the twat who put one in my car! I've still got Calamine fucking lotion in my earholes and up the crack of my ar...." He stopped and changed tack before he forgot. "That's another thing. I want you to find out who did it and sack the bastard."

"Did what?"

"Put that fucking rubber woman in my BMW."

"Did they?"

"I've just said so haven't I. And if I ever find out who it was....!" Pugh made a strangling motion.

"But....I mean how did you get contaminated?"

"Trying to get the fucking thing out of my BMW."

Something occurred to Wainwright. "Oh, that reminds me, on the subject of contamination, we've got problems in the Fruit Gum Department."

Pugh looked puzzled. "Fruit Gum Department?"

"Yes."

"I thought this was an inflatable rubber woman factory? What are we doing making fruit gums?"

"We aren't." Wainwright explained. "I'm talking about the Realistic Vaginal Juices Department. Mr Plimmer told me you'd prefer us to refer to it as the Fruit Gums Department in future."

Pugh treated Wainwright to another glare. "I'd prefer you to stop fucking about and start earning your fucking keep, that's what I'd prefer, Wainwright!" He took a second or two to calm down before carrying on. "And you can start by concentrating on locating a million sets of clothes."

"What?"

"Are you deaf as well as dense? Clothes. We can't flog them as artificial passengers as they are, can we, dressed in fuck all but a bra and knickers. That might be the way they ride about in cars in Ramsbottom, they probably do from what I've seen of them, but it isn't the way they dress in the rest of the country. And keep out of Marks & Spencers and Debenhams, I'm not made of money, get stuff from charity shops, Oxfam and Scoop and that lot, they'll be plenty good enough."

Mention of charity shops reminded Pugh of the time he'd sat in the Commons next to a lady front bencher who was renowned for her habitual use of such establishments. "And try to get stuff that doesn't smell of mothballs. You've got a budget of seven pounds a head, you should be able to fix them up with a tee shirt and a skirt or a pair of jeans for that. And some jackets and trousers, we don't want them all looking the same do we. Get them a hat if there's any change." A thought struck him. "Is there any difference between men's tee shirts and women's?"

"I've no idea."

Pugh stroked his chin in thought. "I'm sure Lorelei once told me that women's tee shirts had extra room built in them for their knockers. Anyway, make sure all the tee-shirts have enough room in them for women as well as men."

"Men? But all the inflatable rubber women are women."

"Now they are. But we're going to have to make half of them into inflatable rubber men."

"Why?"

"Because if every car in the country has a woman in the passenger seat the police are going to get a bit suspicious, aren't they. I know most of them are as thick as a navvy's butty but they're not all stupid."

"And how do you propose we are going to turn them into men?"

"That's my problem."

*

It wasn't, it was Arbuckle's.

When Arbuckle had arrived at an Hour In Bed Wainwright had decided that he would profit most from his four weeks with the firm by spending a couple of days working in each of its fourteen departments, with maybe an odd day in the office. Now in his third week Arbuckle was in his ninth department, the Forming Department, whose function was to extrude the rubber solution into a basic inflatable rubber woman shape.

Pugh had selected this department as the one most likely to come up with an idea for turning half of the one million inflatable rubber women into inflatable rubber men. The task had proved to be quite beyond the talents of the foreman of the department, Mr Greaves, and any of his operatives, so Greaves had delegated the job to Arbuckle in the hope that the benefit of the higher education to which Arbuckle had been exposed would enable him to come up with something.

Before charging the Forming Department with the job Pugh had attempted the conversion himself. The head had been comparatively easy. He simply removed the rubber woman's wig, turning her into an instant skinhead, and added a false moustache and a pair of horn-rimmed glasses. A selection of male wigs in various styles and colours would complete the conversion, in addition to offering customer choice.

Disguising the inflatable rubber women's breasts hadn't been as easy. His first idea had been to let some of the air out, thus making them smaller and flatter. However by the time he'd let out enough air to make them significantly smaller the inflatable rubber woman was only about four feet tall and resembled Gollum out of *The Lord of the Rings* after a night on the mead.

Next he tried to pull the breasts off. However they were stuck on too securely, and when he did eventually manage to pull one off, after much vigorous tugging, it left a breast-sized hole behind. He decided that perhaps gentle persuasion might be a better way of achieving his objective, to coax rather than pull the breasts off. After five minutes coaxing, and with no sign of the breasts coming off, he gave it up as a bad job. But by then, and despite his abhorrence of inflatable rubber women, the gentle tugging of Comely Caroline's breasts had given him an erection. Not wanting to waste it he thought to proposition one of the factory girls - a couple of them weren't too bad if you didn't look at them too closely - but decided against it when he realised that if he were to start fucking the staff physically it would make it that much more difficult to fuck them verbally, if and when it became necessary. At this point he passed on the task to the Forming Department, and ultimately to Arbuckle.

After spending the morning wrestling with the problem, much of it wrestling with one of the inflatable rubber woman he'd inadvertently tied himself to whilst attempting to tie a rope round her breasts in the fond hope it would flatten them sufficiently enough for her to pass as a man, Arbuckle thought he had the answer. Rather than rope, why not a sports bra two sizes too small. Two 40 DD breasts squeezed into a 36A bra. With any luck, and with a sweater on, it would look like a man with a big chest.

He reported back to Greaves. Greaves was not impressed and said if that was the best he could come up with that Mr Pugh would be very disappointed with him, and if Mr Pugh was very disappointed he might very well cancel Arbuckle's stay with An Hour In Bed. At the time Arbuckle had never heard of Pugh, and asked Greaves who he was. Greaves informed him he was the new boss, a Minister in the Government no less.

It was this chance information that gave Arbuckle the idea that would not only scotch VAST's plans to disrupt production at An Hour In Bed, but could well put an end to their activities altogether.

Initially Arbuckle had thought it would simply be a matter

of tipping off the police about the raid. Then he remembered that one of the members of VAST was Seal, an ex-policeman. Who was to say if he were to tip off the police that they in turn wouldn't tip off Seal? In which case the raid would be called off. Possibly to be arranged for a later date when he might not get to hear about.

He could have simply reported the matter to the boss, who at the time he'd first heard of the plot had been Mr Wainwright. But Wainwright himself would probably have told the police, who in turn would have probably told Seal, with the same result.

However Mr Pugh was now the boss. And Mr Pugh was a very powerful man, a Government Minister according to Greaves. Reporting the matter to Mr Pugh would be a different matter altogether. A Government Minister wouldn't just report it to the local police. Government Ministers had friends in high places and it was to high places like the Home Office and Scotland Yard to whom Pugh would report it. And they wouldn't be tipping off Seal.

One thing was certain, he'd have to do something, and quickly. The raid was set to take place in three days time and there was no telling what damage that mad bugger Khan might do once he was let loose inside An Hour In Bed. And Cleaver and the rest of them weren't much better.

Five minutes later he was knocking on Pugh's office door.

*

The most direct way to Pugh's office was out through the back door of the Forming Department then back into the factory through the main entrance. Passing through the entrance Arbuckle noticed an addition to the decor in the shape of a life-size bronze bust of a very ugly man. It was the bust of Pugh, which Pugh had intended to grace his south of

France retreat, but which he had since decided to install in its new location, his idea being that when the workers passed it every morning on their way in it would inspire them to work harder. Arbuckle had never seen Pugh before and when he entered the office he was surprised to see that the bust and his new boss were one and the same man.

"You'll be catching flies in that mouth if you don't shut it," said Pugh.

"Sorry. Sorry Mr Pugh. It was the statue of you in the entrance. I didn't realise it was you."

"Who else did you think it would be but the owner of the factory, Piffy?"

"What?"

"Forget it. Look, I'm a very busy man, what do you want?"

Arbuckle told Pugh everything. How he was a student reading Sex and Inflatable Rubber Woman Studies at Cleek University, how and why he had joined Vigilantes Against Sex Toys, how they planned a raid on the An Hour In Bed plant to disrupt production, when the raid was planned for, why he couldn't tell the police, the lot. After taking everything in Pugh congratulated Arbuckle on his work.

"You've done well....what did you say your name was?"

"Arbuckle, Mr Pugh. Elton Arbuckle."

"Arbuckle. Well what you've done won't be forgotten. You have my word on that. Come and see me when you've completed your studies, I'm sure I'll be able to find something for you."

Arbuckle was delighted. "I'll be sure to, Mr Pugh."

Pugh stroked his chin. "Sex and Inflatable Rubber Woman Studies, eh? What do you do there exactly?"

"We compare the differences between sex with a human

female and sex with an inflatable rubber woman, with the object of promoting inflatable rubber women as an alternative and safe means of sexual gratification."

Pugh smiled. "Well I'm all for that; the more inflatable rubber women we can sell the better I'll like it. But from what you tell me we're not going to have any to sell for much longer, unless we do something about it."

"I was thinking you could maybe bring in Scotland Yard, Mr Pugh?"

"Scotland Yard?" Pugh considered the suggestion briefly. "Yes, good idea Arbuckle. I'll get on to them right away." His eyes narrowed, as they always did when he was up to no good. It was a moment or two before he carried on. "You're well in with this Vigilantes Against Sex Toys bunch of clowns, are you?"

"Oh yes, Mr Pugh. They definitely think I'm kosher."

"Good." He leaned forward in his chair to take Arbuckle into his confidence. "Right. This is what we'll do."

CHAPTER TWENTY ONE

The planned strike on the An Hour In Bed factory by Vigilantes Against Sex Toys was planned with military efficiency. Various duties were allotted. Timings were made. Logistics were co-ordinated. Hammers and crowbars to wreck the factory's plant and machinery were purchased. Chains were procured to enable the ladies to chain themselves to the factory's railings.

There were no problems in purchasing the locks to secure the chains, but the chains themselves were a different matter. Apparently the city of Derby, although rich in the quantity and variety of chain stores, did not have a single chain shop. There may have been shops which sold chains, but Mrs Wisbech, who had taken on the responsibility of buying in the chains, was not able to locate one in the limited time available to her.

In the end she was forced to buy chains from the bondage section of a sex shop, which had gone very much against the grain, but had at least enabled the ladies to take their designated part in the night's activities.

She actually ended up with four chains, one more than the number required, as the sex shop was currently having a sale - *'Everything must go - and you ought to see our vibrators go!'* - and chains were two for the price of one. Mrs Bean suggested that the spare chain could be put to good use by her sister-in-law, who intended to become a member of VAST, and had expressed a desire to come along when she'd learned about the chaining. However Mr Willoughby ruled that as she wasn't yet a member this would be out of order. Furthermore, the extra chain wouldn't be wasted as Mrs Wisbech had indicated that she would like to be doubly chained.

VAST members Willoughby, Cleaver, Seal, Grimshaw, Flannery, Mrs Wisbech, Mrs Bean and Miss Preece were to meet at Willoughby's at 23.00 hours. There they would synchronise their watches. The men would change into combat fatigues and have their faces blackened by Mrs Willoughby with soot from the Willoughbys' chimney. When Willoughby revealed this part of the operation, at the pre-raid meeting at The Grim Jogger, Mrs Bean pointed out that as Seal's house was much more central than Willoughby's it would make more sense if they all met there and had their faces blackened with soot from the Seals' chimney. Seal had seen the sense in this but had pointed out that he no longer had a chimney, so they reverted to Willoughby's original plan.

Much discussion took place before it was finally decided that false number plates would not be necessary. Seal argued strongly for false number plates, making the point that the first question police ask witnesses to a crime is if they managed to get the car's number plates.

Cleaver said he knew where he could put his hands on a couple of sets of false plates.

Mrs Wisbech said she had no doubt he could.

Grimshaw observed that if someone did happen to make a note of their number plates it would only be a matter of time before VAST would be revealed as the brains behind the raid.

Mrs Bean remarked that as she and Mrs Wisbech and Miss Preece would be chained to the railings of An Hour In Bed, holding a large banner with the inscription 'VAST' on it, that the whole world would already know they were behind it.

Mr Willoughby said that in that case it was pointless to go to the trouble of acquiring and fitting false number plates, and that in any case part of the object of the raid was to publicise the existence of VAST in an effort to further their cause. Fr Flannery and Grimshaw concurred. Seal and Cleaver still veered towards having false number plates. Khan said he didn't give a fock either way just as long as he got the chance to go for their joculars. After further discussion, and tea and biscuits, it was decided to stick with their cars' existing plates.

Fr Flannery, who had given himself a night off from purgatory, feeling that travelling in a car for two hours with your underpants full of crushed walnut shells was just a little too much purgatory, then went on to say he had asked for God's guidance. God had told him to gather them all together and pray for them before departing for Ramsbottom. Cleaver said they wouldn't need God's guidance, he knew where Ramsbottom was, he'd looked it up on the AA internet site on his computer and had a print-out of the route.

It was decided that the initial strike would be made on the Forming Department, that being the area in which they felt they could inflict the most damage. Arbuckle, who lived quite nearby, would meet them at the factory gates. After chaining Mrs Wisbech, Mrs Bean and Miss Preece to the railings the raiding party would enter the factory, using the key provided by Arbuckle's university friend. (Two days earlier, acting on Pugh's instructions, Arbuckle had ingratiated himself with Willoughby by telling the VAST chairman that one of his friends at university was at the moment doing post-graduate research at An Hour In Bed.) They would then make their way to the Forming Department and smash up the machines and presses with the hammers and crowbars. Their attention would then be turned to the warehouse, where they would destroy all the stock of inflatable rubber women. To effect this they would use pen knives and carving knives. Khan would use his hook, freshly sharpened.

Having sabotaged all the stock, the original plan had been to return to the factory gates, pick up the women and make good their escape. However Mrs Wisbech pointed out that if things went to plan the ladies would only have been chained to the railings for an hour. As it would be the middle of the night it would be highly unlikely that anyone would have seen them, so what was the point of them being chained to the railings? The decision was made to leave the ladies secured to the railings to see what developed. Willoughby, as the chairman of VAST, would be the nominal leader, but the raid would be led by Arbuckle as he was the only one amongst them who, thanks to his university friend, knew the layout of the An Hour In Bed factory.

There was little chance they would be disturbed. The factory was protected by a system of burglar alarms but Arbuckle knew where they were located and how to switch them off.

As Pugh had forecast, it had then been a simple matter to get Willoughby to agree that it was only good sense that Arbuckle should lead the raiding party. However Pugh had instructed Arbuckle to lead the members of VAST not to the Forming Department, but to the Mixing Department, where they could do little damage. There they would be met by armed police, supplied at Pugh's request by Scotland Yard. Or at least that was what Pugh had led Arbuckle to believe.

The reality was a little different. In view of his plans for the contaminated inflatable rubber women, the involvement of Scotland Yard was the last thing Pugh wanted, and he had arranged for the raiding party to be met not by the police but by a dozen heavies armed with baseball bats (at £500 a pop but absolutely guaranteed to make a few eyes pop, if not hernias, no questions asked), who would then put their baseball bats to good effect by giving the members of VAST the beating up of all beatings up.

*

The two cars carrying the party pulled up outside the An Hour In Bed factory at 01.30 hours, not at 01.00 hours as planned, as the route supplied by the AA website had taken them the long way round as usual.

Immediately they arrived Mrs Wisbech, Mrs Bean and Miss Preece chained themselves to the railings. Then Mrs Wisbech unchained herself from the railings because she'd forgotten to take the banner out of her handbag. Grimshaw offered to take it out for her, and made to take the handbag, but she snatched it away and told him there were things in a lady's handbag that men shouldn't see. Grimshaw wondered if they were the sort of things his X-ray machine had found in his postbag before he'd got the sack, and if they were what was Mrs Wisbech doing with them. Mrs Wisbech took the banner from the bag, Flannery and Seal tied it to the railings, Mrs Wisbech re-chained herself to the railings and the men made for the factory.

Despite being familiar with the labyrinth-like layout of the factory Arbuckle had trouble finding his way to the Mixing Department - things looked different with just the dim light of the interior security lamps to light the way - and he led the raiding party first into the Colouring Department, then into the Breasts Department, then into the Head and Face Department, before finally arriving outside the door of the Mixing Department fifteen minutes later than scheduled.

In addition to the time spent wandering from department to department there had been a further delay when Khan, on seeing a pile of heads in the Head and Face Department, had immediately attacked them and had contrived to get his hook stuck in one. While Grimshaw and Seal were trying to extricate it Father Flannery realised he had forgotten to pray for them, so asked them all to gather round and bend their heads in prayer while he did this. Six heads were then bent in prayer, Grimshaw's, Willoughby's, Arbuckle's, Seal's, Khan's, and the one still stuck on Khan's hook, and Flannery entreated God to watch over their mission.

*

In the meantime Pugh, lying in wait in the Mixing Department with the hired muscle, was going ape-shit. Wainwright, on watch opposite the main gate and in touch by mobile phone, had informed him that the party had entered the factory ages ago. Pugh got him on his mobile again.

"Where the fuck are they?"

"Haven't they got there yet?"

"I wouldn't be asking you where the fuck they are if they'd got here, would I."

"Well it took some time to chain the women to the railings."

"What?"

"They chained three women to the rail...." Wainwright suddenly stopped, then said suspiciously, "Hello, what have we here?"

"What the matter?"

"One of them is coming back." There was a pause, then, "He's heading in the direction of the warehouse."

One of the heavies touched Pugh's shoulder to gain his attention. "I think they've arrived. I can hear noises outside."

"Follow him," Pugh said to Wainwright. "Stop him. Use force if necessary, I don't want him interfering with my rubber women. I'll be there just as soon as this lot's been given what's coming to them."

He switched off the phone and focussed his attention on the raiding party.

*

Outside the door Arbuckle pushed the handle down. He was about to push the door open when Seal wrinkled his nose. "What's that smell?"

Grimshaw inhaled. "I can't smell anything."

"Well I can." Seal's nose twitched. "Smoke? It smells like smoke."

"I can't detect anything either," said Flannery.

"Yes, you're right, I can smell it now," said Grimshaw. "It smells like something's burning."

"It's smoke, definitely," said Seal. "Something must be on fire."

Willoughby looked around him. Then said, somewhat ominously, "Where's Mr Cleaver?"

*

Cleaver was outside the warehouse. Ten seconds earlier he had set fire to it. By now it was quickly becoming an inferno.

Cleaver had decided that simply destroying An Hour In Bed's machinery wasn't enough. Not by a long chalk. All right, it would slow them down a bit, but then what? They'd simply replace the machinery and be making their disgusting inflatable rubber women again in next to no time. More positive action was called for, action that would stop them altogether, not just cause a temporary delay. Fire, that's what was required. An inferno. He had witnessed what the power of fire could do when he'd set the Body Shop alight, and that impressive blaze had been caused with just a cigarette lighter. Imagine the size of the fire a decent quantity of petrol would make!

That morning he had filled 3 one litre lemonade bottles with petrol and stowed them in his haversack. (Willoughby had asked him what was in the haversack and Cleaver had told him he'd packed some sandwiches in case they got a bit peckish. Mrs Bean said that was very thoughtful of him. Grimshaw said he was feeling a bit peckish right now and could he have one, a cheese would be nice if he had cheese, failing that a ham, but Cleaver pretended he hadn't heard him.)

The moment the VAST raiding party had entered the factory Cleaver had quietly detached himself and made his way to the warehouse. He had made up his mind beforehand that the warehouse, where presumably any stock would be held, would be his target. Wasting no time when he arrived there he slipped off the haversack, removed the bottles of petrol and sprinkled the contents on the ground immediately in front of the building. Seconds later he lit a match and threw it on the petrol-soaked ground.

*

Back in the Mixing Department Pugh answered his mobile. "Fire!" screamed Wainwright down the phone. "Fire! He's set the bloody warehouse on fire!"

"Bastards!" screamed Pugh. "The fucking bastards!"

He grabbed the handle of the door and wrenched it open. Arbuckle, his hand still gripping the handle on the other side, came stumbling in with it. Behind him the raiding party saw Pugh and the heavies with the baseball bats. Seal wondered what they were doing there, but guessed it wasn't because they were going to have a game of baseball. The rest of the raiding party didn't have a clue.

Pugh didn't leave them in any doubt. He flung an arm in their direction. "Get the bastards! I want to see some fucking heads broken!"

The twelve heavies burst out of the Mixing Department wielding their baseball bats.

"Oh dear," said Willoughby.

"Bloody hell, I didn't sign up for this," said Grimshaw.

"Our Father, which art in heaven...." said Flannery

"Go for their joculars!" said Khan, raising his hook high and making for the nearest heavy.

"I'm an ex-policeman," said Seal, holding up a hand as though he were stopping traffic.

"You're a twat," said Pugh, and kicked him. He turned his attention to Arbuckle, pointed a finger at him and pushed one of the heavies towards him. "Get that double-crossing little bastard first. Get him good and proper."

"What?" said Arbuckle. "Me? I haven't...." But that was a far as he got as a baseball bat came crashing down on his head and he fell to the ground unconscious.

The battle, such as it was, was all over in less than two minutes; the hammers and crowbars of the raiding party being no match for the baseball bats of Pugh's heavies. Seal was unconscious on the floor along with Arbuckle. The remainder of the VAST members were still conscious but wishing they weren't, as terrible blows rained down on their bodies. Khan was covered in blood. He had managed to pierce a jugular vein but unfortunately it was his own, when the heavy he aimed his hook at had contemptuously knocked it back with his baseball bat.

At the main gate the heat from the warehouse was intense and the ladies, struggling to free themselves from their chains, were now fearing for their lives. The four different locks securing the four chains had four different keys, and all the keys were together in Mrs Wisbech's handbag. When Mrs

Wisbech attempted to free them Sod's Law prevailed and none of the keys she tried in the four locks fitted. Unfortunately when life is in imminent danger logical thinking takes a back seat to blind panic and instead of trying one of the keys in all four locks, which would have eventually brought success, all three ladies tried the keys quite indiscriminately.

Trying to force one of the keys into a lock Mrs Bean dropped it on the ground. Bending frantically to search for it she dragged Miss Preece to the ground with her, whereupon Miss Preece dropped her key too. As they scrabbled around on hands and knees looking for the keys, Mrs Wisbech started muttering a prayer. Mrs Bean joined her.

Abandoning her search for the key Miss Preece started singing 'Nearer my God to Thee'. Their prayers over, Mrs Wisbech and Miss Preece joined her. The irony of the situation, that if their circumstances didn't improve pretty quickly all three of them would be a lot nearer to God than they wanted to be, escaped the ladies.

Just before Mrs Wisbech, finally overcome by the intense heat, collapsed to the ground to join Mrs Bean and Miss Preece, three inflatable rubber women floated past overhead, free as birds, as if to mock them.

A fireman arriving on the scene five minutes later found the ladies in a heap on the ground, quite still. He feared at first that they had perished, asphyxiated by the acrid flames. Mercifully they were still living, but all three ladies were severely singed.

At its height the fire was of such an intensity it could be seen from a distance of ten miles. Cleaver would have been proud. However in his haste to douse the warehouse he had spilled petrol on his clothes, and in the act of setting fire to the warehouse had inadvertently set fire to himself as well. He could be seen from a distance of one mile, but not for long.

CHAPTER TWENTY TWO

The warehouse had burned to the ground in a matter of minutes. Its contents had seen to that. The bottles of petrol by themselves would probably have been enough to do the job, but as most of the warehouse's three hundred and fifty thousand square feet of storage space consisted of highly combustible rubber its total destruction was guaranteed from the moment Cleaver threw the lighted match to the ground.

The vast majority of the one million inflatable rubber women had gone up in flames. However some of them, due to the intense heat, had inflated before catching fire. This caused them to break out, grotesquely, from their charred packaging. The scene as they emerged, many of them dressed in Oxfam cast-offs, resembled something Roger Corman might have dreamed up for one of his horror movies if he'd been trying to go more over the top than usual. One of the inflatable rubber women, wearing a back to front ex-JBL Sports baseball cap, ex-Ethel Austin velour jogging bottoms and an ex-XXL Matalan crop top, was especially gruesome.

Literally hundreds of the inflatable rubber women rose and disappeared into the night air, to be carried far and wide by the blustery north-west wind prevailing that night. Eight sightings of unidentified flying objects were reported from as far afield as Burnley to the north and Lytham St Anne's to the west. Twenty four sightings of identified objects were reported – twenty three were identified as inflatable rubber women; one, which had blown up to immense proportions, was identified, possibly by a drunk, as Dawn French.

During the next twenty four hours a further two hundred

and thirty inflatable rubber women were found within a thirty mile radius of the An Hour In Bed factory. The following day a high ranking police officer went on national television and radio to warn the general public not to go near them as they were contaminated. Twelve men who went to their doctors complaining they were itching all over wished the senior police officer had spoken up a bit sooner.

Three of the inflatable rubber women, welded together by the heat, came to rest in the Harpurhey district of Manchester, and are now in service as a settee. Four came to rest close to Eastlands Stadium, home of Manchester City Football Club. The four City fans who found them took them to the next home match, in an echo of the late 1980's when many supporters of the club took along large inflatable bananas. At the following home game there were over a hundred inflatable women, purchased by the fans especially for match days, augmented by thirty two the supporters already had. A new craze was born, with a consequent boost to the inflatable rubber women industry.

The largest proportion of the inflatable rubber women came down in open countryside, many in farmers' fields. Some were eaten by cows and sheep. The cows and sheep became contaminated and Sir David Donnelly, the latest doom-monger to hold the post of Chief Medical Officer of the National Health Service, misdiagnosed their illness as Foot and Mouth Disease.

Vast tracts of the country were designated no-go areas. The tourist industry complained that the Government was overreacting. Twenty seven herds of cattle, including the herd of a Saddleworth smallholder, and thirty nine flocks of sheep, were slaughtered as a precautionary measure. The price of beef and lamb went up by a third, overnight. Millions of pounds in compensation were subsequently paid out. The Saddleworth smallholder unsuccessfully claimed compensation at a higher rate, maintaining he had lost his lovers. The Government said that lessons had been learned.

The Chief Medical Officer's misdiagnosis was never admitted to. Two months later he was knighted and received an annual bonus.

CHAPTER TWENTY THREE

"I want that bastard Arbuckle sacked!"

"Sacked? But why?"

"Because I fucking said so, that's why."

Two days after the fire Pugh's first action on arriving at the Department of Transport was to phone Cleek University to settle Arbuckle's hash. The previous day he had already instructed Wainwright to sack him if he had the brass neck to turn up at what was left of the factory.

"I can't just dismiss an undergraduate without good reason," said the Vice-Chancellor.

"You can and you will."

The Vice-Chancellor cleared his throat, as if to add weight to his words. "Now see hear, Mr Pugh, I...."

"Otherwise I will pull the plug on the two million pounds a year I have already promised to donate to Cleek University. Of which you will be receiving the first payment in six months time."

The line went silent for a moment. When the Vice-Chancellor spoke again weighty words had been dispensed with in favour of words of a more lighter, accommodating nature. "What did this Arbuckle fellow do, exactly?"

Pugh told him.

Recalling his previous dealings with Pugh the Vice-Chancellor had grave doubts that the university would ever see any more money from the Pugh family, let alone two million pounds a year, but shutting the door on that possibility was not a risk he was prepared to take. Funds for the long overdue replenishment of the university's wine cellar were urgently required, amongst other things. The following day Arbuckle was sent down.

Pugh's second action was to sit back and take stock of the situation. Which was pretty desperate, whichever way he looked at. The warehouse, along with every last one of its precious stock of inflatable rubber women, was no more, completely consumed by the fire. No inflatable rubber women, no artificial car passengers, full stop. About half the factory had been saved from the flames, although what was left of it was severely damaged, much of it lacking a roof. Wainwright had estimated it would be at least three weeks before only limited production would be possible, three months before anything like full capacity could be achieved, and that was pushing it. Previous production levels could be brought about only by the factory being rebuilt and re-equipped. That, as Pugh knew only too well, would take money. Money that he didn't have.

The only good news was that hardly anyone apart from the workforce and the local emergency services knew about the events of two nights ago. And no one but Wainwright and the heavies knew about his part in it. The latter had already been paid and would keep their mouths shut. Wainwright would do the same if he valued his job, and he seemed to have got the message when Pugh had laid it on the line to him the day before.

The blaze had been reported in the inside pages of the Manchester Evening News and three of the daily tabloids, but there hadn't been any pictures. The following day one of the less restrained of the tabloids, true to form, on learning that an Afghan had been hospitalized with a wound in one of his jugular veins, had claimed the involvement of al-Qaida. Another had tried to tie-in the incident with a report of

Martians having landed in nearby Bury the day before. However it had since disappeared from the pages of the press altogether. Fortunately no one at the Department of Transport knew he was the owner of An Hour In Bed as he had been careful not to inform anyone there of his inheritance. Nor, for the same reason, were any of his fellow MPs cognisant. Although nothing would have given Pugh greater pleasure than to shout news of his good fortune from the rooftops, and add "So bollocks to the lot of you" as an encore, he was aware that if he made it public he would have to declare it as a business interest - and his business was his own business, nobody else's. After the general election, when it wouldn't matter what his business interests were, would be quite soon enough to tell anyone.

The police would probably know about it; Wainwright would have had to tell them if they'd asked, and they would have asked, would have 'made enquiries', if Pugh knew anything about the police. But so what? They wouldn't know he'd been there at the time - as soon as he'd made sure the members of VAST were getting what was coming to them he'd made himself scarce and driven back to London. Besides, if it came to the crunch, if somebody claimed he'd been there he would simply deny it; Lorelei would provide an alibi if one were required.

Lorelei knew about it. A couple of nights after receiving his good news he'd had far too much to drink - two bottles of excellent 1982 Clos Rene - and surrendered to one of his regular attacks of boasting. But Lorelei would do as she was told if she knew what was good for her.

Phil knew about it. Pugh considered the problem of the Prime Minister. He would have to be told about the fire of course. Phil was pushing the Single Driver Tax legislation through Parliament and would be expecting his cut from the sales of the inflatable rubber women. But now there wouldn't be any sales, there weren't any inflatable rubber women to sell. Unless.....unless he could come up with another good idea.

He sighed. If it took him as long to come up with a good idea as it had taken him to come up with the artificial car passengers idea he was sunk.

CHAPTER TWENTY FOUR

Arbuckle was bereft. Which was an improvement, as the day before, when the Vice-Chancellor had told him to pack his bags and leave immediately, he had been suicidal.

He still couldn't quite believe it. Three days earlier he had been on top of the world; a young man who knew exactly where he was going, studying the subject of his choice, and with a successful career beckoning. And now....?

During the last few weeks, and in particular since he'd been able to compare having sexual intercourse with a sex doll and with a real woman, he had become more aware, more sure, of what he wanted to do with his life. It was to advocate, promote and encourage sex with inflatable rubber women. It had dawned on him that it was the answer to many men's problems, if they did but know it; the solution to the pent-up frustrations of millions of men throughout the world, if they could only open their eyes to it. He would be the man who would open their eyes; to make them understand that there was nothing wrong with having intercourse with a sex doll, that it was nothing to be ashamed of. He hadn't yet worked out exactly how he was going to achieve this, but he was confident that his further studies whilst pursuing his degree would point him in the right direction. His ambitions had become his dream; and now his dream had been cruelly taken away from him, for without the gravitas the university degree would give him who would listen to him?

When the Vice-Chancellor had informed him of his dismissal Arbuckle had pleaded with him. But the Vice-Chancellor had been adamant. There had been a complaint about his reckless behaviour from no less than the owner of An Hour In Bed, the brother of their benefactor; Arbuckle had brought shame down on the university and that was the end of the matter. It was not something that was up for discussion, there could be no argument.

Arbuckle had come to the conclusion that Pugh must have somehow got the wrong end of the stick in thinking that he'd in some way been responsible for the fire. Perhaps Pugh had got the impression that he'd created a diversion by deliberately taking so long to get to the mixing room? With this in mind he made efforts to contact his boss to try to explain, and having explained to get him to plead with the Vice-Chancellor on his behalf. Pugh hadn't been at the factory when Arbuckle tried to contact him, but Wainwright had given him a telephone number he could try, a London number. Pugh had refused to speak to him. He hadn't even managed to get past his secretary. Arbuckle had pleaded with her, asked her to implore him. A minute later she was back on the line saying that she'd implored Mr Pugh and Mr Pugh had said "Tell the twat if I ever see him again I'll have his bollocks on a plate."

Arbuckle had no alternative but to accept his fate.

*

<u>Minutes of the two hundred and forty third weekly meeting of Vigilantes Against Sex Toys (VAST)</u>. February 18th. Held at The Grim Jogger.

Those attending: Mr Willoughby (Chair), Mrs Wisbech (Hon Sec), Mr Seal, Fr Flannery, Mrs Bean.

Apologies for Absence: Mr Grimshaw (Severe headache), Miss Preece (Depression).

It was felt by Mr Willoughby that Mr Khan would either have attended or apologised for his absence had he not been in the intensive care unit of North Manchester General Hospital. This was duly noted and recorded.

Fr Flannery proposed a minute's silence in respect of the late Mr Cleaver.

Mr Seal seconded the motion.

Mrs Wisbech said that the rest of them could do what they liked but that she was certainly not going to observe a minute's silence since it was Mr Cleaver who had been responsible for leaving her with the complexion of a Red Indian.

Mrs Bean added that she too was against any show of sympathy for Cleaver, for the same reason, and felt that Miss Preece would have been of a similar opinion had she been in attendance.

A vote was taken which resulted in two in favour of the motion and two against. Mr Willoughby's casting vote was in favour and the motion was carried.

A minute's silence for Mr Cleaver was observed. After the minute's silence Mrs Wisbech made the point that she hadn't been silent for Mr Cleaver, she was just being silent because she had nothing to say at the time.

Mr Seal said that made a change.

Mrs Wisbech asked Mr Seal what he meant by that.

Mr Seal told her to forget it.

Mr Willoughby opened the meeting.

Mr Willoughby reported that the raid on the

An Hour In Bed factory, although it hadn't gone quite as planned, had been a huge success. Despite being beaten up it had been well worth it. His information was that production at the An Hour In Bed factory had ceased, and if newspaper reports were correct it would be quite some time before it started again. Fortunately all the gentlemen in the raiding party had been able to get out of the blazing factory before the fire consumed them, unhurt.

Mr Seal said that he wasn't unhurt, he had a broken arm, two broken ribs and a broken nose, thanks to those bastards with the baseball bats.

Mr Willoughby said he meant unhurt by the fire.

Mr Seal said that regarding the beating up they had taken they should report the matter to the police as whoever was responsible shouldn't be allowed to get away with it.

Mr Willoughby pointed out that if they were to do that they would have to explain their presence in the factory.

Fr Flannery said that he too was in favour of reporting the matter to the police as his doctor had told him he might never walk the same again. He suggested that perhaps they could tell the police that they had got lost whilst on a tour of the factory.

Mr Seal said that was all very well but how did it explain the ladies chained to the railings and the VAST banner.

Mrs Wisbech said they could say the reason for

the banner and the presence of the ladies was because they were canvassing for new members.

Mrs Bean said that was an excellent suggestion and in order to add credence to the story she could probably get her sister-in-law to say that the canvassing had borne fruit because she herself had been recruited during the canvassing.

Mr Willoughby wanted to know what Mrs Bean's sister-in-law was doing walking the streets of Ramsbottom at two-o-clock in the morning.

Mrs Bean said she could probably get her sister-in-law to say she was a prostitute touting for work.

Mr Seal said that Mrs Bean's sister-in-law sounded like she was a bit of a sport and he was sorry that Mrs Wisbech had refused to let her be chained to the railings along with the other ladies as she was just the sort of lady member VAST was short of.

Mrs Wisbech asked Mr Seal what he meant by that.

Mr Willoughby reminded Mrs Wisbech that she must speak through the Chair.

Through the Chair Mrs Wisbech asked Mr Seal what he meant by that.

Mr Seal said through the Chair that Mrs Wisbech could take it any way she wanted, he was sick and tired of her bossy ways and she could go fuck herself as far as he was concerned.

Mrs Wisbech told Mr Seal, not through the Chair, that she wasn't going to stay here and be spoken to like that, and left in a huff.

Mrs Bean proposed they should send some flowers to Mr Khan, seconded by Fr Flannery, and the motion was passed.

Mr Willoughby said his headache was starting up again, Mr Seal said he wasn't feeling too good either, and it was decided to end the meeting to allow the gentlemen to nurse their wounds.

The next meeting was arranged for February 25th.

CHAPTER TWENTY FIVE

Hugh Pugh took another sip from his rum daiquiri and contemplated how utterly wonderful life was. Nothing to do all day but lie on the beach getting slowly pissed, back to the five star hotel about five, shag Lorelei, a little nap, then dinner at eight with the local transport chief and his entourage at one of the top Maldives restaurants. He wondered if they had lobsters in The Maldives, he liked lobster thermidor now and again. All day on the beach again tomorrow, getting even more pissed even more slowly as there wasn't an official function to attend that evening and he wouldn't have to reserve some drinking capacity. Then on Wednesday a fact-finding mission to learn about the way The Maldives authorities dealt with transgressors of their rules of the roads – his guess was that they ate them - followed by another afternoon on the beach and an official reception in the evening, black tie.

He turned his head to look at Lorelei, stretched out on the sun lounger beside him, working on her tan. She wouldn't have to work hard, thanks to her daily sessions on the sun bed he'd had installed for her in the attic of his London home, and which had cost him a small fortune.

He ogled her for a moment. Dressed in just the bottom half of the skimpiest of bikinis she was really something. A bit like Britt Ekland before the ravages of time, Rod Stewart, Peter Sellers and God knows how many other lovers had taken its toll on her. They'd only been on the beach for half-an-hour and she'd already caused three men to drool as they walked past on the way to the bar, and to repeat the performance, even more slowly, on the way back.

Pugh didn't mind men drooling at Lorelei. Quite the reverse, he liked them to drool, it proved to him that Lorelei was worth fucking. The day they stopped drooling would be the day he started worrying, the day he started thinking it might be time to turn her in for a newer model. One of the men, Spanish looking, young, the colour of copper, washboard stomach and probably balls like maracas, had actually stopped and openly stared at Lorelei. Pugh had given him a dirty look, just for appearances sake, and shrugged it off. What else could you expect from a dago?

In fact it was Lorelei who was responsible for Pugh being in The Maldives. Six weeks earlier, four days after his dreams for the future had gone up in smoke along with the An Hour In Bed factory, she had asked him just what was his problem, why was he walking about with a face like a blistered kipper? He had almost told her to mind her own business. Women didn't solve problems, they caused them; Mata Hari, Cleopatra, Margaret Thatcher. It was women who had caused his present problem, a million inflatable fucking rubber women.

But for some reason he told her. He couldn't have said why; maybe it was because it was in the back of his mind he'd recollected the saying 'a problem shared is a problem halved'. Not that he thought there was any truth in the saying; he didn't subscribe to homespun philosophy horseshit like that. *"Doctor I think I've got VD." "Well don't worry about it, Mr Pugh, I'll have half of it for you."* Load of bollocks.

It was possibly because he was desperate. Or maybe that by telling her, by talking about it, it might make him feel just a little bit less depressed about it all. It certainly wasn't because he expected her to come up with any sensible solution. But she had. Bless her little cotton panties.

"Is it because of what happened to your factory, Pughie?" she had said.

Pugh snapped at her. "What?"

"Because if that's all it is what's to stop you starting it up again?"

Pugh sighed, long suffering. It couldn't do any harm to tell her, even if it was bloody obvious. "Because it would take money, that's why, my little airhead. Money I haven't got."

"How much do you want?"

He almost told her to fuck off. What difference did it make how much he wanted? She hadn't got any money, silly bitch. But again something made him tell her. Looking back on it now, from the comfort of the sun lounger on the beach of the exclusive Kuredu Island Resort, he could only put it down to fate. God must have been with him. He didn't believe in God, but no matter, he had made him tell her, and he was just grateful to them he had.

A few days earlier, he had asked Plimmer how much it would cost to get the factory back to normal. In the high hundreds of thousands, the An Hour In Bed company secretary had replied.

"A million," Pugh said to Lorelei. "I need a million at least. It might as well be a hundred million."

"I can get you a million, Pughie. No problem."

Pugh looked sharply at her. Was she serious? She looked as though she was, at least as serious as it's possible for a blonde bimbo to look. "Where from?" he said. "Where would somebody like you get a million quid?"

"One of my footballer ex-boyfriends. Maybe not Dwayne, because I hurt him when I gave him the elbow for Shane, but he might, you never know. I mean they like their money, the both of them, if either of them thought he was on to a good thing he'd be in, no messing. Shane would definitely go for it, we parted as friends me and Shane, it was all very amenable, a million's nothing to Shane, he's on a hundred grand a week and that's just wages, that's not counting his hair gel and athletic support sponsorships." She paused, then added, well aware of Pugh's racialist tendencies and suspecting that they might stop him accepting money from a black man, "He's the white one."

She needn't have worried. Pugh couldn't have cared less if Shane were black, brown, yellow or khaki with red spots on as long as he came up with the money. He kissed Lorelei. It was the first time he'd ever kissed her when it wasn't a prelude to sex. A meeting was arranged between Pugh and England striker Shane Hibbert (11 appearances, 0 goals, 4 yellow cards,1 red), for the following day. Hibbert, accompanied and guided by his agent and financial adviser, and having been put in the picture reference the imminent Sole Driver Tax and the undreamed of riches it would bring to the An Hour In Bed operation, agreed to provide one million pounds cash for twenty five per cent of the profits. As with his agreement with the Prime Minister Pugh was confident that creative accounting would reduce this to a figure more in keeping with his idea of what greedy footballers should get for doing nothing more than providing the money then just sitting on their backsides. Five per cent would be about right, call it four.

Work started immediately on refurbishing the factory and either mending or replacing the fire damaged machinery. Six weeks later production began on a limited scale.

A week later the Sole Driver Tax was made law, to take effect immediately. Any sole occupant of a motor vehicle, using their vehicle on a motorway, dual carriageway or clearway, would now have to display a disc on their windscreen, next to the road fund licence disc. The cost of the disc would be one thousand pounds. Drivers failing to display it when using motorways etcetera would receive one penalty point on their driver's licence.

Hedge fund operators, lawyers, council chief executives and all other overpaid people laughed off the Sole Driver Tax. Most of them claimed it on expenses anyway. Members of Parliament weren't allowed to claim it on expenses but put it down as something on which they could claim expenses. A great many of the rest of the driving population, not wishing to cough up a thousand pounds on yet another tax, thought of ways they might get round having to buy a disc.

Pugh, in league with Good, had gauged the response of the driving public well. Getting a point, or even two or three, on their licence was a risk a significant number of them were quite happy to take. The chances of being picked up by the police were pretty remote nowadays, the spotting of a policeman on the outside of a police station being about as likely as the sighting of a Great Bustard.

The An Hour In Bed sales and distribution network were ready for them. The company's mail order sex doll expertise was put to good effect and Male and Female Virtual Passengers (VPs) were added to their catalogue. VPs were also made available at selected supermarkets and branches of Halford's. A leading supermarket had approached An Hour In Bed to see if a 'Value' version could be made available, and talks were well advanced. VPs were advertised in motoring periodicals and leading men's and women's magazines *Loaded*, *GQ*, *Hello* and *OK*. On hearing about VPs the BBC featured them on the BBC 2 motoring show *Top Gear*. Over a hundred viewers phoned it to say the VPs were better looking than any of the three presenters, especially Jeremy Clarkson, and that the VPs in men's clothes were much better dressed. The VPs dressed in women's clothes loaned by An Hour In Bed to the Top Gear team were never returned.

A week before the launch of the Virtual Passengers, Hugh Pugh, accompanied by Lorelei, had begun the previously arranged fact-finding mission to The Maldives. It was touch and go right up to the last minute whether he would go or not. On the one hand he wanted to be around to watch his great idea take off. On the other hand there would be a lot of flak heading in his direction following the introduction of the most unpopular piece of legislation since VAT. On balance he had felt that the avoiding of flak, especially if it meant avoiding it on the sun drenched beaches of The Maldives, was the better option.

He hadn't really wanted to take Lorelei along with him; he was only too aware that once the press got to hear he'd taken his girlfriend on holiday at the taxpayer's expense again they'd be onto it in a flash. But after the way she'd got him out of the deep shit he'd been in he couldn't really see how he could leave her behind. It did cross his mind that with his new found riches about to start flooding in he could pay for her to go, but crossed it so quickly it might as well not have bothered.

It wasn't the only reason he would rather have gone to The Maldives unaccompanied. There were the local ladies to consider. He'd got hold of a Maldives holiday brochure and the girls in it were something else. Talk about dusky doe-eyed beauties. Give him some of that! But with Lorelei on his arm, and his case, there would be a lot less chance of him getting some of that. It would be a great opportunity missed if he were to go on a fact-finding mission to some exotic clime and return home without having sampled a few of the indigenous population -provided of course that he didn't come back with something else as well - and even if he did it wouldn't be something that a jab of penicillin in the bum wouldn't take care of.

There would be opportunities though, he was sure. Lorelei had mentioned a pony-trekking trip she'd love to go on. She would want him to go with her of course; she wasn't daft, she knew that given half a chance he'd be shagging the local lovelies as fast as they could be pulled from under him. But she loved pony-trekking, and if he could come up with a reasonable excuse it would be enough for her to go on her own. He would probably tell her his piles were playing him up, she knew he had piles and how much they sometimes troubled him from the time he'd had them caked in Calamine lotion.

Lorelei suddenly interrupted his thoughts. "Hey, you're in the paper, Pughie. There's a picture." She had taken a time out from sunning herself to catch up with news of home in yesterday's *Daily Mirror*. "I'm not in it," she added, disappointed. She read the news item. "It says I'm with you though. In The Maldives."

Pugh groaned. He could imagine what the news item said.

Lorelei told him anyway. "'*Secretary of State for Transport Hugh Pugh is currently on a fact-finding mission in The Maldives. Where he will no doubt be finding a few facts about his accompanying girlfriend, former Page 3 stunner and ex-Wag, Lorelei Laverne, 37-21-36'.*" She smiled. "Stunner, eh? Nice."

*

Now back living with his parents in Manchester Elton Arbuckle was reading more or less the same news item in his copy of the Times. It was the accompanying photograph which had attracted his attention. He had recognised it immediately as Mr Pugh, the boss of An Hour In Bed. When he learned, on reading the item, that in addition to being the owner of an inflatable rubber woman factory his post in the government was Secretary of State for Transport he didn't attach any great significance to it. He might not know a great deal about the ways of the world, but one of the things he did know was that being a government minister didn't preclude a man from having business interests.

Having neither university to attend nor job to go to, Arbuckle now spent a lot of his time reading the newspapers. So it was almost certain he would read the article heavily critical of Pugh's Sole Driver Tax that was printed the following day. He attached no more importance to it than he had to the discovery that his former employer was the Transport Minister. There were too many cars on the roads, it was a way of reducing them, it sounded like a good idea actually.

It was a couple of days later when he read an article about how some members of the driving public had responded to the Sole Driver Tax that he started to attach significance to his earlier discoveries. Apparently, according to the article, drivers were putting dummies in the passenger seats of their cars in an effort to get away with not paying the tax. There was even a firm selling them, a company that used to sell inflatable rubber women. In fact the Virtual Passenger, as they called it, was not dissimilar to an inflatable rubber woman, according to the report.

It took no time at all for Arbuckle to put two and two together and come up with four.

Arbuckle was not a vindictive man. When he had been

kicked out of university he had entertained no thoughts of revenge. It was just his bad luck, an unfortunate chain of events, Mr Pugh mistaking his true intentions, whatever. However after learning that Pugh was profiting from his position in the Government in an illegal way, or if not strictly illegal as near to illegal as made no difference, he began to look at things in a different light. For this was the man who'd had him kicked out of university and ruined his future. And was now making a mint from his dubious dealings. And as if that wasn't enough, while the mint was being made, he was sunning himself in The Maldives with his beautiful blonde girlfriend. And all paid for with the taxpayers money.

Arbuckle thought about the situation long and hard. For what he'd done, and especially what he'd done to him personally, Pugh deserved everything that was coming to him. The trouble was that what was coming to him at the moment was all good. How could he make it bad?

CHAPTER TWENTY SIX

"'....*Plumber Derek Hargreaves leapt in the canal after he heard the mother of the eighteen-month-old scream for help. Hargreaves, 41, said: 'She said she couldn't swim. I'm not a very good swimmer myself but I couldn't just let him drown. Another passer-by gave the toddler the kiss of life following his rescue in Winsford, Cheshire.*'"

Lorelei looked up from the newspaper to see if Pugh was taking any notice. He wasn't, as usual. She didn't think he would be. Why should he, he hadn't taken any notice for three weeks. She looked at her watch. She'd been reading to him for fifty minutes. Ten minutes to go and her hour would be up and she'd leave him to it. She was about to start reading the next item of news in the paper when the nurse walked into the room. She smiled at Lorelei and indicated Pugh. "Still asleep is he?"

Lorelei nodded, glumly. "Are you sure this is doing any good, Nurse?"

"It's not so much the reading as the sound of a familiar voice."

"It's really boring." Lorelei sighed deeply, as if to back up her words. "I usually only have five minutes with the paper, that's plenty for me."

"At least you're a caring enough person to read to him. I remember one patient's wife making a tape recording of herself talking and we had to play that all the time," the nurse said, with a disapproving raise of her eyebrows.

The day after the news of Pugh's jolly to The Maldives had appeared in the newspapers he had caught Dengue Fever. The tropical disease, not unusual in The Maldives, initially manifests itself as a rash. At first Pugh thought it was a return of the infection he'd picked up off the contaminated inflatable rubber woman and had sent Lorelei out for a bottle of Calamine Lotion. The Maldives, one of the most fragmented countries in the world, is made up of one thousand one hundred and ninety two islets, and after visiting half a dozen of them Lorelei soon discovered that not only were chemists shops thin on the ground in The Maldives but that Calamine Lotion was even thinner.

By the time she returned three hours later, tired and Calamine lotion-less, Pugh's condition had deteriorated considerably. He had broken out in a fever, had a blinding headache, and every muscle and joint in his body ached. Lorelei sent for a doctor, who took one look at him and despatched him by power boat to the Indira Gandhi Memorial Hospital at Malé.

Although Dengue Fever can be a very painful affliction most people fully recover from its effects within in a week. A very few die from it. Pugh did neither, but after four days lapsed into a coma. After a further week had passed all traces of the fever had gone but he was still comatose. He was to remain so for six weeks.

The hospital doctor had suggested to Lorelei that if she were to play some of Pugh's favourite music it might help to coax him out of the coma. However Lorelei wasn't aware of Pugh's musical tastes, or even if he had any, in fact she very much doubted if he liked any sort of music at all. She knew lots of music he didn't like; that rap shite, that hip-hop shite, that girl band shite, that boy band shite, Leona fucking Lewis and Lady fucking Gaga, because whenever they'd come on the car radio he'd told her she could switch that crap off and right now unless she wanted to get out and walk. So in lieu of any favourite music Pugh might have had she played her own favourites. There had been no reaction from Pugh at all, except for the time she put a James Blunt CD on and he made a gurgling sound and one of his knees jerked.

The doctor also told Lorelei that reading to Pugh might help. Perhaps if she read from his favourite books? As was the case with music she didn't know his favourite books, or even if he had any. The only things she'd ever seen him reading were restaurant menus. She tried reading the menu from one of the local restaurants but gave up after five minutes as it was making her feel hungry. Thereafter she'd settled for reading him the *Daily Mirror* every day, or the *Sun* for a change.

After checking on Pugh, the nurse left, and Lorelei picked up the newspaper and carried on where she'd left off. "Here we go again, Pughie. 'During a quiet period at the Marylebone premises of Madame Tussauds Waxworks yesterday ....' "

Deep in the Land of Nod Pugh heard nothing.

CHAPTER TWENTY SEVEN

"Are you sure?" said Wainwright, in disbelief.

Arbuckle nodded. "Oh most definitely."

"But half the stock are females."

"I thought that chap....what was his name?....Arbuckle....I thought Arbuckle's undersized sports bra idea had solved that problem?" said Arbuckle.

"Well it could, but...." Wainwright stopped, still very doubtful about the whole business. "You're quite sure about this, are you? I mean we've only just started production using the existing moulds."

"Dad was quite insistent," said Arbuckle. "I only spoke to him this morning about it - he's on a fact-finding mission to The Maldives you know - he said you're to effect the change just as soon as is humanly possible."

Wainwright saw a snag. "But half the clothes we've purchased are for women."

Arbuckle was ready for this objection too. "Transvestites. Dad wants half the Virtual Passengers to be transvestites." Arbuckle eyed Wainwright anxiously as the factory manager took in his words.

During his time at An Hour In Bed Arbuckle had had little contact with Wainwright and the factory manager hadn't recognised him when he'd presented himself, a few minutes earlier – the moustache, horn-rimmed spectacles and a ginger wig had seen to that. However acting wasn't his strong suit and he wasn't at all sure he'd be able to pull it off. So far it had all gone to plan but Wainwright was still looking far from convinced. "Your father didn't say anything about this to me before he left," the factory manager now said.

Arbuckle gave a rueful smile and shook his head. "Dad can be a bit forgetful sometimes. It's all the responsibility he has as Secretary of State for Transport, in addition to all the hours he has to put in here at An Hour In Bed. Busy, busy man my father."

Wainwright remained suspicious. "Actually I didn't know Mr Pugh had a son."

"Oh yes, I've been working as Dad's PPS ever since he took over at Transport."

"Well he never told me."

"Have you got a son, Mr Wainwright?"

"As a matter of fact yes."

"You never told me."

"My son isn't asking me to totally disrupt production."

It had taken Arbuckle two days to come up with a way to exact revenge on Pugh. His first thought had been to set fire to the factory again. It had worked once so why not twice? He reasoned however that Pugh might suspect who was behind it and return his revenge in spades. Pugh couldn't have him booted out of university again but he could have him beaten up again, and he was still hurting from the last beating.

One of the many ways he thought he might get back at Pugh was to desecrate the MP's bronze bust that now stood in the entrance to the An Hour In Bed factory. Spray paint it or defecate on it or hack at it with an axe or something. But although that would have given him a certain satisfaction he recognised it for what it was, just a petty act of revenge and not worthy of him. And not severe enough. He wanted something more devastating.

It was a clue in the *Times* crossword that finally gave him what he was looking for. Immediately after thinking about vandalizing Pugh's bust Arbuckle had taken a break from his thoughts of revenge and turned to the crossword for a little light relief. 1 across was '*Where Andrew Motion waxes lyrical? 6,8*'. Arbuckle solved the clue in no longer time than it took to read it. 'Madame Tussauds'.

The answer brought memories of the waxworks flooding back; it had been years since he'd visited it, he was still a boy. He recalled the attractions there; the Chamber of Horrors; the stars of stage, screen and television; the famous politicians. And it gave him his idea.

Now, in Wainwright's office, with Wainwright still dithering, Arbuckle took the bull by the horns. He took an envelope from the inside pocket of his jacket, took out a letter and placed it on the desk in front of Wainwright. The letter heading, produced on Arbuckle's computer the night before, read '*The Department of Transport*'. In smaller lettering, underneath, were the words '*From the Office of The Right Honourable Hugh Pugh, MP*'. The short typewritten message below read '*Wainwright. Do as my son Jeremy says reference the new moulds. Or you'll have me to answer to when I get back.*' It was signed Hugh Pugh.

Arbuckle was sure he'd got the tone of the letter right, it was written in the straightforward, bombastic, domineering way that Pugh always spoke. But he'd had to take a chance that Wainwright had never seen Pugh's signature. Apparently he hadn't, for having read the letter Wainwright nodded, and said: "Well if that's what he wants, that's what he wants I suppose."

Arbuckle smiled. "It is, Mr Wainwright. And I'll be sure to let Dad know how co-operative you've been."

CHAPTER TWENTY EIGHT

Six weeks to the day after going into a coma Pugh came out of it, to the sound of Lorelei's voice on a tape recorder reading a four weeks old Daily Mirror.

Lorelei herself was in Spain. Three weeks earlier she had flown the coop. The time she'd previously spent reading the newspaper was spent on even more beach time, but now without the forbidding figure of Pugh by her side. It had taken only the slightest encouragement from her to attract the Spaniard with the washboard stomach. He turned out to be a footballer, Jose Maria Oloroso, a creative midfielder with Real Zaragoza. It wasn't very long before he was being creative with Lorelei's midfield.

Pugh found out that Lorelei had left him two days after he had left hospital and returned to the hotel where they'd been staying. She'd left a note, telling him she'd fallen for the creative midfielder, but not how creative he'd been. Pugh could have guessed. He wasn't over bothered about Lorelei walking out of his life, it had been very nice having her to fuck whenever he felt like it, but a fuck was just a fuck after all. He was getting a bit fed up with her anyway and a change was overdue. Besides, he had more important things to think about, more important things to do. Such as getting back to England and spending some of the fortune that had been mounting up from the sales of Virtual Passengers all the time he'd been in a coma.

Within an hour of regaining consciousness Pugh had put through a call to Wainwright at An Hour In Bed. Yes, they were back in full production. They couldn't make Virtual Passengers fast enough. Sales were going through the roof.

Pugh booked the first available flight back to London.

*

Phil Good had returned to London twenty four hours earlier, following a two week trip to Washington to shore up Britain's special relationship with the United States. The Prime Minister was not a happy man. The talks with President Sole had gone well - Sole had agreed to let Good carry on unconditionally sucking up to him – but in his absence things had not been going so well for him back in Britain. Things had gone so badly in fact, according to the phone call from the Deputy Prime Minister, that he'd been forced to cut short his visit a day early and return to Number 10 immediately.

*

When Pugh arrived back in England it was close to midnight. As it was Slaithwaite's day off he was forced to take a cab from Heathrow to London. When he was settled in the back of the cab the driver, with a cheeky grin on his face, asked him if he didn't think it would be more appropriate if he sat alongside him in the front. Pugh had no time for cab drivers, especially cheeky ones, and asked him if he thought it would be more appropriate if he shut the fuck up and got on with his job. Perhaps if he hadn't, perhaps if he'd asked the cabbie why it would be more appropriate if he sat in the front, and the cabbie had told him, it would have saved him from having the shock of his life the following day. But it wouldn't have saved his neck.

*

Before travelling up to the An Hour In Bed factory, where it was his intention to inspire his employees to produce Virtual Passengers in even greater quantities than they already were, Pugh had planned to call in at his office at the Department of Transport. However the Prime Minister's secretary phoned him whilst he was still eating breakfast. Pugh was to get his arse round to 10 Downing Street faster than shit off a shovel. Those were the words she actually used. Pugh knew immediately that he was in trouble. It wasn't the first time she'd said those words to Pugh. The first time she'd said them he had asked her who the hell she thought she was talking to. She had replied that she knew precisely who she was talking to and that Good had told her to use those words exactly.

On this occasion he just asked her what sort of trouble he was in. She told him deep, deep shit sort of trouble, shit so deep he would be lucky if the top of his head poked out of it. He didn't persist. Phil had probably told her to say that as well.

Slaithwaite picked him up ten minutes later for the short drive to Downing Street. When being chauffeured Pugh occasionally sat in the front passenger seat. You got a better look at young girl's bottoms in the front than you did in the back. With the prospect of facing a wrathful Phil he needed cheering up and the sight of a few pert young bottoms would fit the bill very nicely.

On the way to Number 10 he thought he saw Slaithwaite glance at him with the same sort of silly grin the cab driver had on his face the night before. However he didn't say anything, he was probably mistaken, a minute earlier he'd thought he'd seen Phil Good in the passenger seat of a Ford Fiesta, and there was no way that the Prime Minister would demean himself by travelling in such a modest car. Besides, it was travelling in the opposite direction to Number 10, and wasn't the Prime Minister already there, waiting to give him a roasting about something or other?

Pugh himself was at Number10 a few minutes later. On walking into the Prime Minister's office he hadn't known quite what to expect. He could have taken a guess, but a million guesses wouldn't have got him even close.

"Good morning, Prime Minister," said Pugh, on entering. He always addressed Phil as Prime Minister when trouble loomed. "I got here just as soon as I could."

Good just sat and looked at him without saying anything. If Pugh had been a piece of shit, or a Conservative, the Prime Minister couldn't have looked at him with more revulsion.

Pugh broke the silence. "Er...what is it I can do for you, Phil....Prime Minister?"

"Don't you think you've done enough," Good spat out, adding a generous layer of vehemence to the revulsion.

"I'm sorry?"

"You fucking will be."

Good indicated the antique leather chesterfield against one of the walls. Pugh looked over at it. For a split second he thought Good had a twin brother. And that he himself had a twin sister. But only for a split second. Twin brothers and sisters aren't made of rubber. One of the figures sat on the settee was the image of Good. The other looked very much like himself, but dressed in women's clothes.

"Fuck me," said Pugh, his eyes almost popping out of his head.

"I intend to." Good flung an arm in the direction of the rubber twosome. "Look! You've made a fucking laughing stock out of me, Pugh."

Pugh didn't really know what to say. He tried a conciliatory approach. "Yours is quite a good likeness, Prime Minister."

Good went berserk. "A good likeness? It's the spitting fucking image of me!"

Pugh made another attempt to mollify the Prime Minister by pointing out his own even worse circumstances. "At least yours isn't dressed up as a woman."

"That one isn't. Thousands of the buggers are." He jabbed a finger at the Virtual Passengers. "Those fucking things are riding about in the passenger seats of cars all over the country. All over the fucking country, Pugh."

"Shit," said Pugh.

"You might well say shit. Jesus Christ, we didn't stand much chance of being re-elected before but we've got no fucking chance at all now." Something suddenly dawned on him and set him off again. "My memoirs are going to look good now, aren't they, by Christ are they. *'Phil Good - the Rubber Years'*." He shook his head. "That's if any publisher will want my memoirs now." It reminded him of another mortal wound. "And what about the lecture circuit? Who the fuck is going to want to listen to me give a lecture now? You've fucking ruined me, Pugh, fucking ruined me."

Pugh opened his mouth to speak but Good beat him to it.

"Fuck off out of my sight."

*

At that very moment Arbuckle was having a pre-breakfast quickie with Bouncy Beyoncé. Seated side by side on the settee in his bedroom, as though watching the performance, were Virtual Passengers in the images of the Prime Minister and Hugh Pugh. They were souvenirs, or perhaps trophies, mementoes of Arbuckle's revenge on Pugh. As he rolled off Bouncy Beyoncé a minute later he caught sight of them. It bought a smile to his lips. It always did.

When Arbuckle had come up with the idea of producing

Virtual Passengers with the faces of Pugh and the Prime Minister he hadn't for one moment thought it would be the ruin of Pugh. He'd simply been trying to put a spanner in the works until such time as Pugh found out about it and put a stop to it. More a dig in the ribs than a kick in the bollocks. As things turned out Pugh would have happily accepted a hundred kicks in the bollocks, and might even have agreed to castration with a rusty can lid, if only what had happened hadn't happened. Pugh catching Dengue Fever and not returning to England for a further six weeks was a bonus. Along with the happy coincidence of Good leaving the country for America, the day before the new Virtual Passengers went on sale, it meant that thousands upon thousands of them had swamped the country by the time they'd returned to England. Even non-car drivers were buying them, just for a laugh.

Arbuckle allowed himself another smile as he recalled the details. Once he'd hit on the idea the rest had been easy. Even the potentially difficult part of his plan, stealing the head of the waxwork figure of The Prime Minister at Madame Tussauds, had been achieved without any bother. He already had the head of Pugh, on the brass bust at the An Hour In Bed factory. He had been able to get into the factory with the key he still had from the time of the raid by VAST and knew how to make moulds from his time in the Head and Face Department. A piece of cake. Bob's your uncle and Fanny's your aunt. His smile grew broader. And he was Pugh's daddy.

EPILOGUE

The day after Pugh's return from The Maldives the Prime Minister dismissed him from his position as Secretary of State for Transport. Pugh tried everything to save his job apart from going down on his knees and begging. When all his pleas fell on deaf ears he went down on his knees and begged. When that failed he prostrated himself on the floor and begged. All to no avail.

Although deeply disappointed Pugh was not immediately too concerned about his future. After all he would have the income from the inflatable rubber woman factory. The models had been changed back to the original designs and sales were still very healthy.

However Good hadn't finished with him yet. A month later he had the Sole Driver Act repealed, with immediate effect. A week after that a letter from Good's solicitors arrived on his desk. It alleged that Pugh had defamed the character of the Prime Minister of Great Britain, by depicting his face on to what was to all intents and purposes an inflatable rubber woman, and that Good was going to sue him for every penny he had.

By this time, with thousands and thousands of Virtual Passengers left on his hands, Pugh hadn't got many pennies.

Very soon after he had no pennies at all, plus a severe cash flow problem, when creditors started pressing him for the payment of bills and the Inland Revenue and VAT people sent final demands for the outstanding taxes that still hadn't been paid.

A month later, following further pressure from Good, Pugh was declared bankrupt and An Hour In Bed forced to close its doors. Two months later, at the general election, Pugh lost his seat.

He has been unemployed ever since, but is on the waiting list for a job at Carpet World, having told them he knows a lot about carpets.

It soon dawned on Arbuckle that if he could fool Wainwright into believing he was someone else then he might be able to fool the people at Cleek University too.

Wearing a ginger wig, a moustache and glasses might not be convincing enough though. Five thousand pounds from his parents' savings to fund a little plastic surgery to his nose and jaw made his disguise much more convincing. Putting his computer to good effect again he supplied himself with a false identity, put his new name on his qualifications, and once again successfully applied to Cleek University. He is now in his second year there. He and Bouncy Beyoncé are still together.

Vigilantes Against Sex Toys is still in existence. However, following the debacle of the raid on the An Hour In Bed factory, they have reverted back to a policy of friendly persuasion in their efforts to discourage people from using sex toys.

Printed in Great Britain
by Amazon